PLAGUE

SOUL

BY: MATTHEW W. FENN

I want to dedicate this book to all my readers. As long as you keep reading, I'll keep writing! Blessings!

Contents

CHAPTER 1

Darkness. Void of warmth. Mixtures of pain and grief over what once was. Torn, distraught landscape that could not be warm even in the embrace of the red sun. Trees reached out like witches' fingers, void of any vegetation or life. Their blackened, shriveled branches were not unlike bone showing through a small layer of flesh beneath the surface. It was as if the fingers meant to grab the sun and steal off of its life-giving qualities if only to claw at the ground for a moment more. The fresh rain in the otherwise foul landscape had moistened the soil of the swampy, putrid-smelling grounds.

Coldness settled as empty huts and buildings were callously quiet. The only noise was of the cold ripping wind that traveled the spine of anyone who stood out in the open to experience its wake.

The wizard pulled his hood closer to himself as another frozen wind sought to deplete what remained of his warmth. He breathed a heavy breath. Steam poured from his crimson-bearded face. His cheeks much resembled his hair in color as blood rushed to compensate for the temperature.

He tucked his leather gloves into his side as a shiver went through him. His golden brown eyes searched for any hint of life. Despite his searching, there was nothing that indicated such.

He approached a dilapidated shack where two figures grabbed at a hefty form. Their bird-like masks were ashen with gleams of white and silver. Their crooked beaks turned to him inquisitively. With the same quickness, they disregarded him at the notice of the sage brown robes that he wore. The symbols sewn onto his cloak were notable by most. A symbol of an owl on his breast with outstretched wings highlighted his intention. When the light fell upon the cloak, the eyes of the owl reflected gold.

The plague doctors moved jerkily and grabbed each end of the form and tossed it into a nearby ditch. It was with that movement he noticed the dirt on their forearms and sleeves. A steady smell of dried herbs and spices came from their beaks in the form of thin smoke. The closer he drew, the more aware he was of the stench.

He shook his head with disdain at their practices.

Magic was magic.

The doctors bent to grab another heap of weight when he motioned for them to stop. Their glassy eyes in their tilted heads again perceived him as they stood in watchful silence. He pointed to the spot in front of him. They seemed to comprehend as they moved silently and gently placed the bag neatly in front of him and then moved back as if giving him an offering. Their eyes gleamed.

There was a single line of knitting that merged the bag's sides together. He knelt down and pulled at the finely woven string. It zigzagged free until there was a wide line. A bitter smell wafted through the newly made hole.

He pulled it open to reveal the pale, ghastly face of a young woman who looked to be sleeping. Black sores and lesions were painted along her thin face; the bones hid her age, but he knew from experience how it ought to have been seen.

He shook his head and stood back up. He looked at the doctors who were still regarding him in a frozen, statue-like state.

He motioned and covered himself again with the edges of the hood of his robe. They moved almost like they were made of air, picking up the body and bag with precision. They approached the pit and simultaneously picked up long metal rods. They lifted their silver padded bands to the tops of the diamond ended rods. The inner chambers of the rods were aglow with emerald green fire. They dipped their rods into the newly-formed large pile of bodies.

Green flames poured out from the diamonds like water and engulfed all around in scattering emerald embers.

His eyes watered at the new smell. He resisted the urge to lift his hand up in front of his mouth. He moved over to the shack as the doctors seemed to move in a lax slow-motion, as if they were in no real hurry.

The wooden door was old and rotten, so as he pushed it open he felt the wood almost give before him. The walls were beaten down. The once fresh mud-brick looked to be losing its intended structure. For building standards, it was quite large in stature.

A straw mattress bed lay in its center, and one wall held a long-ago burned-out hearth with stones that had shifted out of place. The thatched roof above was scattered with holes and gaps. He noticed the darkened stain and an indentation on the bed where someone had lain. He pushed through other objects. Whether it be an open dowry chest or scattered pieces of debris, he gave a dissatisfied look as there seemed to be nothing of interest. He began to turn to leave when a gleam caught his eye. Under the bed, he found the source of the shine.

He knelt down next to the small object that was no bigger than his palm. A broken vial lay scattered with powdered residue. He eagerly grabbed the powder with his gloves and carefully removed a small vial from his robe and poured it into it. He continued the process until one-third of the vial was filled with residue. He tucked it into his pocket without a noise and proceeded out of the home.

He placed his gloves into the green fire that had begun to shrink in size in the ditch. He watched the flames as he pulled his gloves out; the fire hadn't hurt them, but there was no longer any powdery residue.

He fixed his gloves back on his hands and watched the doctors going about their solemn work. A sense of certainty took him as he reexamined the vial.

The doctors had acted strangely around him when he had first met them.

A strange meeting it had been.

Talk had always been that they were actual bird creatures under their shapely masks. He wasn't sure because their behavior was certainly sporadic, and bird-like in movement.

He had never heard them speak, but when he presented his purpose of investigating the sickness, they listened intently without reply. Many wizards had told him they had heard them speak words, but he was certain he heard clicks and other strange noises as they breathed. *There wasn't anything more strange nowadays.*

He tucked the vial carefully into his pocket and looked around the village that had once been known as Beresh. A thriving location, it had been one of the many domains of the realm -- a realm that held old names. The Land of the Witch Trees had always been desolate, but somehow it seemed more so now. This village had always been excluded from that sentiment.

Death took no exceptions.

He shook his head as he turned south.

There was someone he knew who would be able to tell him what he needed.

CHAPTER 2

Anwar Lioneyes grasped the reins of his horse. The red stallion snorted as they neared the gates which were made of polished stone and mortar. On its corners were watchtowers that stood as warnings to any that got too close. He pulled down his hood and took in a long breath. It was a change of scenery, very much different than he had grown accustomed to over the course of many months of travel. His horse clopped along the dirt road.

Soldiers opened the gate. Their bodies were adorned with the same crested owl that he himself bore. He encouraged his horse forward.

The keep was full of multicolored stones. The base was made up of stones larger than his horse. They continually wound into a spiral-like structure overlooking even the gate towers themselves. Jutting up from them were gardens and courtyards that reflected the green of the cloak on his shoulders. He disembarked from his horse as it neighed before moving to the stables on its own whim and course of pattern.

He watched it go as he walked the cut path of stone stairs. He was greeted by several passersby but only gave them curt nods and flat smiles. He was not big on exaggerated greetings.

The two giant doors groaned and creaked as he placed a palm onto the impression where a door knob would normally have been. The doors opened inward, as cool air poured out into his hair. Even so, the room was well lit with torches that continually burned. Books of every age, color, and condition lined what seemed to be endless bookshelves that twisted with the tower of immeasurable height. Floor upon floor extended out of view.

He sighed as he knew he needed to ascend to the very top to speak with whom he intended. He chuckled to himself as he remembered the last time he had made the mountainous climb. He trudged up the steps with purposeful speed. He could feel his muscles begin to cramp and burn. The steps themselves were steep and required those using them to extend their gait. The wizards who had built the hold had said, "Knowledge requires straining away at the goal." He snorted as he stretched again.

He looked around. There was scantily a sight where someone didn't have their nose buried in a book or scroll. Stacks and stacks of reading materials were scattered all around them. If not in a book, they were arguing among themselves about something they had read or debating material. He smiled thinking about it.

He couldn't help but unintentionally eavesdropping on a conversation on what would win in a fight, a wraith, a ghost, or a spirit? He shook his head because honestly he couldn't definitively tell the difference between the subjects.

A place of learning, indeed.

As he moved further along, the social status of those inside began to change. What was once those who wore fine and expensive robes was replaced by plain and often dirty looking dress. He also noticed that those further up were not as adequately groomed as those below. They even looked tired and more wearied. That wasn't too far-fetched, he thought, considering how high up they were.

He paused as he realized that he was at his destination. In his people-watching, he had made way more progress than he had realized.

The door jutted off from the nearly top level. He paused, looking at the door. An odor wafted from the cracks around it. He sniffed. Was it lilac? Flowers?

He shook his head.

Whatever it was, it was familiar, but somehow unknown to him.

He pushed the door and peered in.

Towards the far end of the room was an elongated table which appeared as if a library had thrown up on it. Books were cast here and there and scrolls drooped from the table as if they were looking for the opportunity to jump to the floor away from the hoarded mess. He looked over to the bookshelves and saw only a few books that were neatly placed there.

He shuddered thinking about trying to delve through the mess. Behind the pile of books sat an aged wizard who looked as used and ancient as the books he was flipping through.

The wizard had a deep onset scowl as he bit down on a wooden pipe. With an expression like he was looking at something too far away, his face was a flurry of wrinkles along with striking blue eyes behind circular glasses perched on his nose. His mangled, long salt and pepper hair was a striking comparison to Anwar's own neatly trimmed beard and head.

This wizard looked like he should have been looking for a book on something called "scissors."

The wizard wore the same robes that he did, but where as he had kept his maintained, the other wizard's were faded and crusts of mud were on the hems and edges.

"I've told you a hundred times that you need a new robe."

The wizard's sharp glance made him hesitate. The anger shifted to a kind and happy expression as it occurred to him who was speaking.

"Ahhh," he stretched, "I thought you were the bookkeeper again." He chuckled.

"Anwar," he removed his glasses, "Anwar Lioneyes. Good to see you again."

He pushed away from the table.

"You have been gone for some time." Anwar smiled and motioned.

"There has been a lot that has kept me busy here lately." The wizard cleared his throat.

"A wizard is always busy," he waggled his finger, "Or he's dead." Anwar wasn't so keen on the expression or its meaning, but nonetheless, he nodded in agreement. He didn't enjoy arguing the legitimacy of something that didn't make much sense to him. It was often like chasing a rabbit down a hole with this wizard.

"Too true, but I have a need for you, Elric Shatterblade," he said with decorum.

"Elric Shatterblade," he gave him a mirthful grin, "For you to use my full name means you mean to flatter me and ask for a favor."

"Or I'm a parent," he chuckled.

Elric snickered.

"As you know, I've been to the far north, searching the land of the crooked trees and the so-called Dark Mages. I have found something that I long suspected but I still need confirmation from someone with more experience in the field. Your knowledge of alchemy and potions is unchallenged."

As if on cue, the potion that had been sitting beside Elric bubbled over and shattered to the ground simultaneously. The smell of lavender and lilac scented the room.

The smell was no longer a mystery.

Elric simply turned a sidelong glance to it and shrugged his lack of concern.

"The place needed to smell better anyways."

Anwar resisted the urge to rub his temple. He knew his eye had to be twitching if not for the fact that the air was now making his eyes water.

"Look no further," Elric said, stroking his own beard.

Anwar reached into his pocket and withdrew a small vial.

The black grainy powder had clouded at the top as if it were giving off a gaseous substance.

He handed it to Elric who looked at it with hungry eyes.

Elric held it carefully despite his shaking grip. He tapped his fingers lightly on the glass.

"Where did you find this?"

He held the vial up to eye level and shook it gently.

"In an abandoned hut in one of the now deceased villages." The old wizard rubbed his beard with his free hand.

"More specifically, I was sent to investigate the strange sickness that befell so many there," Anwar added. Elric bit the corner of his lip.

"So they're all dead, then?" his voice was uneven.

"The raven doctors have been sent. They have been at work purifying the vast area to be sure of no further spread."

Elric sat the vial down after pushing some books out of the way.

"What do you suspect?"

Anwar put his hands in his pockets.

"I believe it is the direct result of extremely dark magic -- magic once thought lost when the Scourge Wizards were eliminated." Elric raised a brow, "You think so?" Elric looked deep in thought.

"What were the conditions of the bodies? Did they have reddened spots? Growths? Lesions or boils?"

"Black lesions. Lesions that sapped them of their life's energy. They looked like skeletons when I saw them. Shadows on the ground."

"Plague powder then," Elric said, casting a dangerous look to the vial.

Anwar's jaw hung slack.

"Plague powder?"

He nodded, "I would require some tests but based on what you have told me it is irrefutable. For the doctors to arrive means that they take it seriously."

Elric waved his hand over the top of the vial. A spark shot from the corked stopper.

"This should seal it for the time being. You are fortunate it did not explode in your pocket."

Explode?

"The powder is volatile. If contained, it explodes and would therefore have infected you. You didn't touch it, did you?" Eyes of scrutiny observed him now.

"No, I'm not unseasoned in these things. Nor am I that foolish. However, I had no notion that it would randomly explode on me ... so there's a chance I'm not as qualified as I originally thought." Elric's nose scrunched, "Live and learn."

"So, what or who makes plague powder?"

"Not Scourge Wizards … that much is unlikely. They may have been strong, but they weren't intelligent enough to come up with something on this scale of things. No, this is the work of something more macabre, something with darker magic even than their foolish dealings."

"You're sure that it wasn't someone who just happened to stumble upon the spell and used it unwittingly?"

"Again, it's possible, but not likely. For this powder to be as fine as it is would require incredible knowledge and intention. The technique to make something as potent as this would mean they intended it and that they knew what they were doing, considering they did not infect themselves in the process."

Elric grabbed a cloth and tightly bound it around the vial. He fastened a ribbon around it. Anwar couldn't help but notice he was shaking all the more.

"We must take this to the Warlock. I know that he will be able to help us identify the source and also spread the word of this deadly plague that you have encountered."

He put the vial into his bag and patted it.

Anwar agreed, running through his mind the necessary preparations that would be needed for the long journey that they would undertake.

His mind raced as his attention fell back onto the liquid that was now staining the floor.

"One question before we leave."

Elric had begun moving around books and scrolls but stopped.

"What exactly were you doing with this potion?" He pointed to the broken glass.

He chuckled.

"I was researching a permanent scent-changing potion. Did you notice how the room smells like lavender and lilac?" Anwar couldn't help but smell it again.

"Yeah."

"Well, if I did it correctly, the room should smell this way forever." He narrowed his eyes.

"Why would you do something like that?"

He gave him a look as if it were strikingly obvious. "Because it stinks in here. Sweaty mages read day in and day out with no concern for hygiene or anyone else's nostrils." Anwar rolled his head. He could sympathize with that.

"So what if it spilled on us?"

Elric smiled a smile that showed he was missing a tooth.

"Well, I hope you would enjoy smelling like a beautiful flower for the rest of your natural life."

Anwar pointed at a stain on Elric's robe.

He made a "tsk tsk" noise as his face looked smug.

"That's why you ask."

CHAPTER 3

The smell of lilac and lavender floated from behind Elric as Anwar followed him. He looked down and noticed other smaller stains all along Elric's green robe. Anwar couldn't help but laugh to himself about the idea of an old wizard smelling as if he had spent the afternoon swimming in flowers. He moved to the right to avoid the now overwhelming perfume.

They made their way to the stables. The horse he had arrived with had been replenished of goods by the stable master, who greeted them with familiarity before going about his business. A telling shovel of stench accompanied him.

Elric's horse was an old mare that had a mane as wild and as unkempt as the old wizard's wild beard. The horse huffed and stamped its feet twice. Its muscular white legs tensed.

"What's wrong with you?" He gently patted her head and stroked the rim of her nose.

Probably smells different to her.

Anwar jumped onto his own horse with no effort.

"She is probably confused as to why her rider smells like food she might eat."

Elric gave him an aggravated look and groaned as he climbed the stirrups.

"Better that than to smell like this place."

He tightened his reins as he fidgeted with the pack behind him.

Anwar knew better than to ask the question, but his own curiosity got the best of him.

"Why that scent in particular? Wouldn't it be more intriguing to smell like the woods, or even the ocean?"

The old wizard straightened up after moving around to make himself more comfortable.

"In aromatherapy, lavender and lilac can be used to treat a number of ailments. Not to mention make people sleepy."

"Ah," was all he could muster.

Their horses whinnied their excitement as the gates opened up to the hills and trees surrounding the hold. Their hooves pounded against the rich grass and dirt.

"Doesn't really help you to stay inconspicuous." Elric didn't respond, no doubt trying to think of a rebuttal.

The guards that stood on either side of the exit gave them simple nods as they passed into the tree line. Moments later, the guards gave each other weird looks as they motioned to their noses.

The fresh air was soothing and warm. They both were taken aback at how beautiful the trees looked against the sun.

"It's been awhile since I've seen such a nice day as this," Elric said cheerfully.

It was in that moment that it occurred to Anwar how pale the wizard looked.

"Do you think the Warlock will set up a reward for any information on the powder?"

Elric bobbed up and down with every step of his horse.

"I hope he does. Though it's his decision. Any information we can get will help."

He agreed.

"How did you discover the sickness?"

Anwar cleared his throat.

"I was riding to Zaolith to study the scrolls there in regards to a particular spell I've sought after for some years. On the way, I heard rumor of a peculiar disease that killed in a matter of days. A man wanted me to see his wife after I found the source of the story; knowing I was a wizard, he thought I might be able to do some good."

Anwar looked away from him to the road ahead of him. "It was something I had never seen before, so I sent word to the Healers of Occulae and proceeded to the Witch Trees to the north. What I saw there was ... terrible to see."

Elric nodded.

"How did you know you wouldn't get sick?" Anwar shook his head.

"The raven doctors examined me and found no indication of infection. Besides, you know that I'm a light wizard."

A light wizard was a special type of magic caster. Light wizards never got sick, and along with being able to cast fire and light spells, were especially rare. To be a light wizard usually equated to riches and services in the court -- none of which suited Anwar. That's what made him unique, not just his magic.

"I had them examine me to be sure. Despite it all, I didn't want to take any unnecessary chances."

"That is always wise."

The pass bent as they rode along. After the bend, a river babbled next to them with a soft mumble. The trees thinned out some and the water became wider and clearer. Their silhouettes reflected on its crystal-clear surface.

During the several hours they rode, Anwar relayed the details of the infected, and Elric listened intently and quietly, asking small clarification questions here and there. Finally they reached an old looking bridge of wood and stone. They went over it and headed a few miles before they came to a clearing far enough from the river.

They both tied their horses and Anwar started to gather kindling for a fire. He went around until he had plenty to sustain them and cleared a spot. He piled the kindling into a cone shape and pulled out a knife and flint. He struck it at its base. Bright orange flames curled around the wood and turned red and yellow. Fresh smoke wafted up as the fire popped. He bent down and breathed into the small flames until the fire was built up to his satisfaction.

Elric looked at him as if he were a book to be read.

"Why not use your magic?" he pried.

Anwar smiled and put away the knife and flint. "Because, I don't want to abuse magic. It's often too easy

that way. If I can't make a fire without magic, what would I do if I found myself unable to use magic anymore?"

Elric inclined his head.

"I guess when you put it that way ... it makes sense. I often mix potions by hand instead of using magic to assist me."

He let out a breath as he sat on a downed tree.

Elric fidgeted into his pocket and pulled out a small rectangular book. Its cover displayed ancient writings -- words that were unidentifiable. Elric opened it to a page and after another moment turned to another, his eyes searching and twitching.

"Ah!" he said and passed it to Anwar, holding the book open to the intended page, "Read this."

He took it from him and was surprised at how deceptively heavy the book was despite its size. He tenderly grasped the burnt pages in his fingers. They felt like a moth's wings.

"Be careful with it. I grabbed it from the library before we left. It is of immense worth. I doubt anyone knew it was hidden in there."

"What is it?"

He gave him a mirthful glance before looking back towards the book as if gesturing. The words were faint but legible.

To call it a cruel death is an understatement. Black powder is a cruel powder that if it were to come into contact with skin kills indefinitely. Magic users seem exempt. The cruelty of this sentiment seems to suggest this manufactured plague exists for the sole purpose of eliminating those ungifted with magic. To think such an idea could even begin to grow into one's mind is inconceivable. The hatred involved is manifested in the cruelty that is the death involved with those infected by the powder. Plague powder is still much a mystery as to how it is created and to its extent in magical properties. The shining black sand exudes a gaseous substance, that if contained could at the processor's dismay combust and infect even non- and magic users alike. It is then assumed that blood contact is what causes infection of even wizards.

Anwar flipped the page as the author of the book continued to speak of the powder on a more chemical level, seeming to marvel over its coarseness and substance, but nothing more that was interesting.

"How did you know that it was a powder?" Elric asked, "I only knew through reading this book once a year ago. I was looking for some unique mixtures and stumbled upon it."

Anwar shrugged, "Through all my searching it was mentioned that there was a powdery residue and I noticed it since I knew to look for it. That's when I thought of you. You are knowledgeable about these things."

"There is no doubt in my mind now," Anwar said, "This is definitely the stuff."

Elric smiled.

"There is one point of contention I have. Who was the author of this book?" He motioned towards it.

Elric shrugged, "Whoever it was used a pseudonym, but it's held knowledge ... supposedly ... that he was a raven doctor. The name is lost to me. This is a dead language on the cover. It's almost like he or she didn't care for us to know. It's mostly unimportant to the author."

"Why was the inside common language?"

"Who knows? Maybe the author wanted it that way. I, for one, believe it's a spell. So only certain people can read it. It would make sense that not too much is known about it. It smells of magic even."

"Are you sure the author is a reliable source?"

"Hmmm."

Elric put the book back into his cloak and warmed his hands. The flames danced shadows across his face.

"So?"

"Whoever they are, they are."

"They?"

"It's believed it's the culmination of several people's works." Anwar rested his arms on his knees and gazed into the fire. "Elric, I know you've told me how old you are but, do you

remember much about the plague wizards?" He pursed his lips.

"I remember the sickness they brought. They wore bones and shrouded their faces. Except for their purple eyes. There's not too much else to say, but I am only a mere 300 years old."

Anwar shook his head.

He was to turn 30 soon.

"What of their magic? Are they only able to use the powder?" Elric moved uncomfortably on the log.

"Their magic is based around absorbing life force. One such tactic is the powder. Through this means they are able to do unnatural things. Through this they can be almost immortal."

Anwar rubbed his beard again.

"Then why are there no more of them around?" Elric's eyes brightened.

"An excellent question. Are you aware of polar opposites?" "Yeah, like hot and cold, or fire and water?" He nodded.

"Plague wizards take, while other wizards, such as you or I, give.

Our magic comes from our own abilities. Plague wizards must take life in order to access their magics. Only natural wizards can truly contend with them. Most other wizards who can only employ books to use spells would find themselves robbed of magic. Not forever, mind you, but long enough for them to succumb to death."

"So, we are the bane to them."

"Exactly."

Anwar threw a log into the fire. The flames crackled and sparks floated into the dark.

"I'm surprised you weren't taught more about them." He shrugged.

"Only that they lived some time ago, and that they were bad beings."

Elric snorted.

"History is important. I'd love to know what was deemed more important than such an essential piece of magical history."

"That's why I have you," he said as he poked at the fire. "Besides, knowing me, I probably wasn't listening."

Elric chuckled.

CHAPTER 4

The unnamed village lay before them destitute and bare as their horses whinnied. The houses were empty shells with not even a single candle or source of light to brighten the windows. The houses themselves were scattered and looked to have been made some time ago. There were signs of age with unknown brown material clinging to the roofs of the habitations. They all seemed to be sinking in upon themselves.

Anwar urged his steed forward regardless. "Melina doesn't like this," he said as he rubbed his horse's snout. Her nostrils flared with short, rapid breaths.

Elric turned up his nose. His horse, whom he referred to as Brolin, took hesitant steps. Her nervous tittering made the ground rattle.

"Animals have senses that you and I do not. Be cautious;

something is wrong here."

They proceeded single-file through a space between two huts.

"Do you smell that?"

"Yeah, I'd recognize that odor anywhere." "Dead," he said simply. His face was stone.

"They've been dead for awhile, I'd wager."

He jumped down from Brolin with Anwar mirroring him.

Elric motioned to the pit that had been dug some distance away.

Charred black remains were almost indistinguishable. Except they both knew. "Doctors' work."

He agreed and turned to the closest house. The door hung on what seemed to be a little of the hinge. He pushed with his shoulder and it dropped in a heap of dust and soot. The horses snorted and flicked their tails sporadically.

Elric rummaged through remains with a piece of debris.

He felt a stale heaviness inside once he stepped into the hut. It was dark and smelled of mold and mildew. The moisture inside made it more humid than it had been outside.

His hand moved out of habit to his nose without him noticing it. He summoned a fiery orb of light that buzzed around the room in quick, jerky movements. Its hum was soothing to him.

He gasped.

Fungus and black growths covered a mass in the corner of the ruined room. The skull's mouth was agape as the same fungus had grown through its mouth and throat. The body itself looked thin, with spots of bone and thin pieces of recognizable flesh. The air grew heavier the closer he got. Its arm was petrified as if it were trying to reach for something or maybe even ward something off.

Anwar coughed roughly and swallowed. The stench was so dense that he doubted his hand was doing any good for it. He turned away from the smell and pinched his nose.

"Elric, come here," he called.

Elric continued to rummage through the pile and lifted an object. He turned to Anwar, who gave him a quizzical look. Anwar pointed at the corner without removing his grip on his nose and now mouth.

Elric dusted off the object and put it into his cloak.

"What is it?"

He looked through the doorway.

"Oh," was all he sputtered as he walked over.

He put a hand into his pocket and produced another vial and knife. He took a breath and stepped inside. With the side of the blade, he scraped on the flesh in the corner. The noise was wrenching to their ears, as the blade scrubbed deeper into bone. The skin was hard and rough.

After Elric seemed satisfied, he sealed the vial and openned the door over the entrance as he ushered him out. He tucked the vial in his cloak along with the orb.

"That powder caused all that?"

He nodded.

"Prolonged, the plague itself devours flesh and turns into a parasitic fungus, such as in there."

Elric tossed the knife to the pit.

"Doctor fire is sufficient to cleanse the plague ... so far. There may be more to the story as time progresses."

He paused as he pulled out a melted piece of metal.

Anwar couldn't believe it.

"A doctor's mask?"

Elric bit his lip.

"Why would one of them be in the burn heap?" He shrugged.

"The doctors have always been ... er … reclusive. You never see them without their masks. I have never in all my days seen one without it. It could be that one of these got sick or ... maybe ... something else."

"Something else," he muttered to himself Anwar crossed his arms.

"This is one of the worst cases I have seen in my travels. To think how many have been affected already is concerning."

Elric cast him a saddened expression.

"It is evident we must make it to the Warlock sooner than-" A loud thump interrupted him.

They both looked in the direction of the noise and back at each other as if to ask, "Did you hear that?"

The broken door shifted from the doorway trim.

Thump.

They gave each other shocked looks.

Thump.

The door rattled and a hissing whisper came from the darkness of the doorway.

"Surely not," Elric stammered.

Thump.

"Elric … do they only burn bodies to stop the spread of disease …?"

Thump.

The door shook quicker.

"Or ... something else."

Elric pulled back his sleeves and folded them around the insides of his elbows.

Anwar drew a pale dagger from his belt.

The magic within him made the blade shine in silver-white light. A heavy noise dropping made the door fall completely from the opening in a crash. They both took shallow breaths and looked intently into the impenetrable dark.

"Heeeeehh," the thin voice whispered.

They both were wide-eyed as the hairs on their bodies stood on end.

"-Eeeeelp meeee," it groaned in a more hoarse voice.

White fire sprang onto Anwar's wrists as he called to his light magic. The fire surrounding his wrists began to spin and rotate at the crackle and pop of intense heat he was pulling from within himself.

Elric's palms exhibited a similar display, with bright blue electricity forming at the base of his palms. Magic arched randomly up and down his arms.

The voice in the dark took a long, labored breath. "Whyyyyy diiiiid-nnnt yyyyyyoooou heeeeelp meeee?"

Thump.

The creature's face pushed back the darkness, revealing the skull-like face that appeared to grin hungrily. Fungus wrapped itself around the bones, the growth itself holding its jaw in place. The jaw seemed to be hanging in an uncommon position, and moved up and down unnaturally. Its teeth clacked together in clicks as he took breaths. Its body was thinner than it should have been to support such a creature, but its empty eye sockets seemed darker than the blackness around it. *Thump.*

The air was heavier now that the monster edged forward more and more.

Neither wizard dared to move.

"What is that?" Anwar asked through clenched teeth, his fists tightened.

The words came out as more of a growl than a question.

"I-I don't know," Elric said, pale.

The fungal creature tilted its head at the sound of their voices. Its jaw dropped loosely as it let out a nasty fluid that had been caught between its clanking breaths. The disgusting aroma of the dead was more intense and burned their noses. Behind it as it crawled was a dark trail of mass as its legs were inoperable.

"Heeeeelp meeee …." it said in more of a demand than a plea.

Anwar positioned his knife, adjusting his grip. The white glow ignited more rays of brightness. The outline was like an eclipse against the sun.

"That may not work," Elric said, his features now more angular and terrifying in the light of their magic.

"It's worth a try."

Anwar struck the ground with as much power as he could in a rumble of ground and stone. As the knife made contact with the ground it sent forth a shockwave of fire which moved along the ground like water and surrounded the creature like a mighty snake. The fire struck out but sputtered into smoke and ember, with a noise like water being poured onto a fire.

Black steam rose from around the creature.

"Saaaaaaave meeeeeee," it complained as it kept crawling forward.

The attack seemed to have only agitated it further.

Anwar tucked away the blade as he released his magic from him in a growl.

"How did you know it wouldn't work?" Elric's face never left the creature.

"It was a guess. Seeing as there are dead doctors over there, mind you that I have never seen die before, this could lead one to believe magic may not be effective against whatever killed them."

"How many more?"

"Dozens. That was just one mask. The rest were completely in pieces. There are many more bodies. Something was responsible, and I am sure we have found the answer to that question."

Elric's electricity moved like squirming snakes around his forearms.

"Your electricity is still magic."

Elric took a step forward, "I don't intend to attack it with it." The creature slunk forward as black steam kept pouring off of it.

A wall of electricity cycled until it was a wall of lightning above their heads.

The creature reached out with a greedy expression. Its fingers burned as it touched the barrier.

A cry of displeasure resounded from its mouth. Its face looked more sidious.

"Noooooooooo," it said hoarsely, "Heeeeelp." Anwar dusted off his robe.

The creature let out a long, exhausted groan.

"So how do we kill it then?"

Elric rubbed his beard.

The magical barrier began to shrink as the creature touched it again. It shook faster and more jittery-like. Its body was more jerky than slow and methodical.

The barrier shrunk at a more alarming rate.

"It's magic," Elric said in a whisper.

"What?" Anwar asked as he clenched his fists so much that his knuckles were white.

"We need to go. NOW."

Elric waved his hand and the barrier disappeared.

"To the horses."

He turned, followed by Anwar to where the horses were thrashing against their restraints. The alarm was clear as their wide eyes were accompanied by the clapping of their hooves against the clay ground.

Against the noise they could hear ever so clearly the "thumping" drawing closer and closer with each passing moment. Raspy breaths made shivers go down them as they mounted the bewildered horses. They moved the restraints as the horses voiced their terror and uncomfortableness with snorts and pawing at the ground.

As they beckoned their horses forward, neither of them looked backwards; they could almost feel the raspy breath against their necks on the worn path. Anwar could feel gooseflesh all over him as he thought better of sneaking a glimpse.

CHAPTER 5

"I've never seen anything like that!" Anwar exclaimed as he leaned into his horse.

The morning sun's light had begun to peek over the monstrous trees on the horizon.

"Neither have I ... neither have I," Elric said haggardly. They had ridden the majority of the night. Every noise sounded suspicious or like the creature that they were sure was still following them. Neither they nor the horses had received any much-needed rest in the meantime. Their pace made them sore and stiff.

"There has to be some sort of explanation. Doctors have NEVER been killed, like you said. You said you saw dozens of them. Do you

know what this means? *Dozens* of doctors dead. This is serious! Worse than any plague you or I have ever seen!" Elric nodded and swallowed dryly.

"As I told you, doctors have a special magic to deal with sickness. Their magic purges it, eradicates it, and ensures that it will not find a foothold any further than the fires spread to engulf it. To see they have succumbed to death only means their magic failed; that the plague was stronger. That serves as an explanation as to why we had no success with our magic."

Anwar made a silent scowl and rubbed his eyes.

"So this could be a result of a powerful spell? Magic made this?" The old wizard pursed his lips and dipped his head.

"Magic has always been a benefit to everyone that uses it. It has been corrupted to do something unimaginable. That 'thing' was feeding on our magic like you or I would feed on bread. I've seen people grow old and grow sick; I've seen real sickness and watched many die in my lifetime. I have *never* seen something that drew upon magic in this way. It's like it was leeching on the very fabric of our power."

Anwar slowed the pace of his horse by easing back on his reins. "There was nothing about this thing in that book? Or the archives?"

"Nothing to account for this," he said dully.

He knew it to be true, as he knew the old wizard had combed through the sources several times over. He was vastly knowledgeable on many subjects. To see him have nothing more to say scared Anwar more than he had been.

"This, whatever it is, is new."

"Why did you summon guardian lightning when my arch-flame failed?" Anwar asked.

"I wanted to see for myself. At first I wasn't certain if it was just fire in general since doctors use a type of fire magic to cleanse those who have passed on due to sickness. I wanted to see if another form of magic would affect it or if it was magic overall."

The trees around them thinned out significantly. Although the once large trees were now giving way to smaller ones, the trees lacked lower branches, so it was easier for them to ride at a leisurely pace. The undergrowth itself seemed to change into soft moss instead of briars and weeds.

The horses themselves slowed down to enjoy the comfort of the shade and the soft underbrush.

"So, if it feeds on magic, how in the world can a wizard kill it?"

"It's simple," Elric took a swig of water from the waterskin, "Kill it without magic."

He put away the skin and removed from his pouch the vial containing what he had recovered from the creature. The flakes shifted around in the vial as he shook it lightly.

"Let's make camp here," he motioned with the bottle. "The horses could use the comfort, and the ground will be good for our own bedding." They disembarked and allowed the horses to move around freely to munch on the lush grass and moss. They happily hummed as they ate their fill with chomping mouthfuls of green.

Within moments they had a modest fire that warmed their bed rolls as they sat in a haze between consciousness and sleep.

Elric carefully cooked some salted beef and began cutting vegetables. His gaze never left the two vials that he had placed nearby him on his own bedroll. Anwar, meanwhile, had his eyes closed.

His eyelids were tightly shut as he mumbled under his breath with both hands out in front of him.

Elric dumped the cuttings into the pot. The water steamed and bubbled. Soon the pleasant aroma of the stew made the air rich. He sprinkled herbs and spices into the boiling water.

Anwar opened his eyes and rubbed his hands together. The smell of food broke him out of his trance of casting wards and spells.

"That should be enough to protect us. Or if nothing else, let us know when someone comes around that shouldn't." His eyes hungrily gazed longingly at the pot.

"It's hard to focus on spells when a smell as good as that is there

to distract you."

Elric chuckled.

"I will take that as a compliment. This old man knows some things about cooking; it's just a potion really if you think about it. A vitality potion at that."

Black herbs floated on the surface of the water.

"It still needs some time to absorb the spices." He stirred. "While we wait," the old wizard said, "there is something I would

like to do."

He left the pot and grabbed the vials with wrinkled hands. He removed a strip of bark from a tree with ease and sat it down in front of him to use it as a makeshift plate.

He carefully poured one of each vial on opposite sides of the bark.

Anwar edged away from the bark but focused on what he was doing.

The way he positioned them showed that he was being careful of not allowing the two substances to touch.

"May I have your dagger?" Elric asked with a smile.

He repositioned the corks back into their respective openings. Anwar shook his head and passed him the dagger more out of curiosity than anything.

Elric took the dagger carefully, treating it as if it were hot or something fragile. He tilted the blade towards his index finger. He pushed the tip into the middle of the tip of the finger. A drop of red blood came from the prick and stood still on his finger as he guided it over the essence of the creature. He squeezed it with his thumb.

The blood dripped into the blackened flakes. Once it reached the black it hissed and stirred like angry ants. They vibrated for a moment and became still again.

Anwar's mouth went slack.

Elric tilted his head and repeated the process again. This time he squeezed his finger over the plague powder.

The drop fell, but nothing happened when it dripped into the powder.

"Hmmmm," Elric said as he rubbed his chin.

"So? What does that mean?" Anwar asked, transfixed.

The old wizard wiped off the dagger and passed it back into his open hand.

"What do you think, Anwar?"

Elric bit his knuckle and made a clicking noise with his tongue.

Anwar shrugged.

A light popped inside of the old wizard's eyes.

"I need you to take a drop of blood from one of the horses."

He raised a brow. He obliged without a word because he knew that this was going somewhere ... hopefully.

He didn't want to offend his own stead, Melina, but instead pricked Brolin while simultaneously petting her snout. The horse was none the wiser. He moved the fresh blood over to Elric.

"Put some on the powder."

He tilted the blade and the moment the blood hit the powder it hissed and shook like the other blood had made the creature substance.

"Now this," Elric pointed to the other side of the bark. The blood dropped into it and this time nothing happened.

Elric looked satisfied with himself.

"You can wipe off the dagger now."

Anwar complied.

"So you've seen it; now what do you think?"

Anwar knew the way he phrased the question meant that he already knew the answer but was merely testing him. The old man's shining brown eyes looked whimsical.

"Magic?"

Elric looked both impressed and satisfied with his answer. "Yes!" he exclaimed. "It seems we are dealing with two strains of

the plague."

Anwar put a hand to his chin.

"A way to target both magic and non-magic users?" He nodded.

"Normally we wizards need not fear plague or sickness due to the magical capabilities that flow through our blood. You see, the normal person has a quality in their blood that fights off infection or fever, and with magic we have an added ability to combat anything that would do us harm in that sense. We are resilient to most afflictions. That is why a wizard can never get a cold ... well for the most part ...."

Anwar nodded, following along.

"Unless the sickness is born of magic! A 'magical' disease!" He pointed to the bark.

"You see, whoever created this doesn't care who lives or who dies. It's a plague for both magical and those who are not. We aren't dealing with someone who hates one or the other."

Anwar narrowed his eyes.

"But why make something like that? Why go through all the trouble?"

Elric shrugged, "For you or I to answer that, I imagine we would have to be completely batty."

Anwar came to a realization.

"So we can become infected."

Elric waggled his finger.

"Exactly."

Anwar shook his head and edged away more from the bark.

"So how do we intend to destroy it, then?" "Not magically, I can tell you that."

"Could they be destroyed by their opposites then?" Elric's jaw was the one to drop this time.

"And they say wizards lack common sense. What an idea, my boy. It's worth a shot."

The stew bubbled as if to suggest it didn't think highly of being ignored.

"After we eat, of course."

CHAPTER 6

The smell of cooking meat made him rise from his slumber. The sweet aroma made him feel like he was floating. His stomach gurgled his intention as his hand gently covered it.

"Good morning! Rise and shine."

Anwar straightened his robe and moved to a sitting position.

He noted Elric's unkempt hair and beard which only looked slightly more messy than the previous day. The bags under his eyes were now a darker shade.

"You stayed up all night?" he asked as his eyes drifted towards the sizzling sausages on the flat of a rock over the fire.

Elric motioned for him to have some. Anwar gathered some and took a bite. The grease layered his beard and he apologized at his ravenous appetite. He wiped it away.

"Yes," Elric said, holding up his finger, "What you said last night intrigued me. So much so that I concocted a few ... er ... well ... a lot of tests."

Anwar swallowed, feeling the burn of having eaten too quickly. "And?"

The roof of his mouth felt numb at both his eagerness and heat of the food just coming off of the fire.

Elric clapped his hands together, giving him a look as if he should have known better.

"I used a fire spell on the powder and it burned to a crisp. Nothing was left. However, it produced a gas which made some of the plants grow like the fungal creature we saw a few days ago."

Anwar nodded and was concerned he had slept through something like that. For him to not stir when he was a light sleeper was rare. He must have been exhausted. That or his trust for Elric meant he was at ease. "Magic itself, when used, can catalyze it to dangerous effects," the old wizard took a bite of sausage, "so I tried several methods until I resolved to pour water on it. After all, water is one of the greatest forms of magic."

He motioned as if he had an invisible watering jug. "The fungus shriveled and died immediately."

"So that creature at the house didn't leave shelter because of …."

"Rain or water, exactly."

Anwar chewed thoughtfully, "So the importance of a thorough bath hasn't lost its value."

Elric winked, "Water rids of most disease when applied. Hand washing isn't a new concept, but it could be life or death nowadays." He tilted his head and nodded.

"Much as plants require water and sunshine, I believe these things need darkness and maybe a host?"

Anwar stood up and stretched. A few muscles burned as he leaned backwards. He let out an elongated yawn.

"You shouldn't have stayed up all night. For what you found, though, I can't be mad."

Elric sighed.

"Sleep can be easily obtained, answers cannot."

Anwar came to the horses. They were lounging on the ground chewing on small pieces of grass. They eyed him with sleepy expressions.

He pursed his lips to see more "prick" spots on Brolin. He shook his head and tossed them both an apple. He patted Melina's nose.

"Can animals get the plague?" he asked, scratching behind her ears.

Elric poured water over the fire, causing it to steam and hiss. "I'm not certain, but I don't see why they couldn't."

Anwar studied her yellow and brown eyes as if he expected to see something different.

"I hope not," he said, thinking of how long she had traveled with him. She had been his only companion for hundreds of miles.

"If it were possible, we would have no hope to combat it. There are nearly ten times the amount of animals as there are people in this realm alone."

The wizard waved his hands.

"Birds would fly and spread the infection before we even knew we had been taken; imagine if mosquitoes had it!"

"I see what you mean."

Elric waggled a finger at him.

"That would be an unimaginable horror, and something we need to keep in mind. We can never really know what new magic cou-"

A strange look overcame Elric, something undefinable behind his old blue eyes. Whatever it was caused him to turn and look at him because his line of thought had suddenly ended. Anwar tilted his head questioningly.

His mouth was open. He looked away as if he were trying to look at something a good distance off.

"Disable your wards," he said with a firm voice. Anwar swallowed roughly at his unexpected tone. *Disable the wards?*

"Are you ready to go?"

Elric was moving around quickly as he grabbed the bed sacks and folded them. He slung them on the horses, tying them without precision. He hurriedly scooped up smaller items into packs and in one motion kicked dirt over the smoking remnant of their campfire. Embers turned into fireflies at each kick. He was tense.

Anwar looked around confused at the calmness of everything around him. Besides that of the old man in front of him.

"Do it now!" he said with a readable alarm in his face.

Anwar obliged with the squint of his eyes, reaching out to his wards. There wasn't anything strange about them at all. He could feel the steady magic that was holding them up. The words to disarm them poured at as easily as water as he followed instruction.

"It's done," he said after the last word left his lips.

Elric continued moving around sporadically. He tied more bags onto the horses.

Then he began pacing back and forth as if he had forgotten something. "Care to tell me what's up?" Anwar finally said with a fist on his leg.

Elric pulled at the straps.

"Get on your horse. *Now.*"

Anwar felt he shouldn't doubt the seriousness of it. Whatever would cause him to be unhinged wasn't a joke.

He got onto the horse as he reached for the horse's mouth.

"What is it?" he asked, wrapping the reins in his fist.

Elric started muttering to himself as he, too, put his feet into his spurs.

Whatever he was saying was unrecognizable.

"Go. Now," he said in more of a quick whisper.

The woods were silent. Birds that had once been chirping were now nowhere to be heard. Even the light breeze had all but stopped. What had once ruffled leaves in the tall trees did not move at all.

It was then that he realized he hadn't been paying attention to his surroundings enough.

Elric looked as pale as a ghost as he summoned a sapphire orb of fire into his palm.

Anwar felt tightness and heaviness in the air. He had never experienced anything that made the air he breathed feel so thick. The fiery orb shot away from them with a "bang."

It flew out of their view into the trees, which shook around where the orb traveled. Anwar watched and strained to see the strange figure nestled under the trees. The hair on the back of his neck stood on end. Whatever had spooked Elric had good reason to.

CHAPTER 7

Again, the once densely populated trees thinned out. The same was true of the comfort that they had provided with their cover. The soil itself turned from a dull brown to a pure black which looked rich -- but the lack of growth denied it. The loud clop of their horses' hooves told them the ground was densely packed. Trees that were clinging to this ground looked withered, and there was very little green to be seen. Boulders and rocks were littered around them randomly.

Off in the distance were tall mountains looming over the horizon. The air itself was cold, as they had traveled north a great amount. Neither had kept much track at the pace they had moved.

"Did we lose whatever it was?" Anwar asked, his breath visible against the chilling breeze.

Elric clutched his hood against his face to avoid the soul-ripping cold. "We dare not stop to find out."

Anwar let his vision drift over the inhospitable landscape. There was no single wisp of cloud in the sky, which was a rust color that seemed to never change despite the passage of time. This made it difficult to determine how long they had been riding in the area.

"It can't be that fast ...." Elric muttered as he pointed to the horizon, "The stone field ends soon. Once we enter the Wraith mountains, we can rest. Only until then, we have to put some water between us."

He let out a long breath.

The old wizard told him that he believed the creature had followed them and found them because of his wards of protection. Something inhuman as that thing in the rubble was something he wanted far from his mind, and more importantly himself.

The horses were tired, as they had gotten no sleep in the days they had ridden.

They had slowed halfway through the first day when they had spotted the dark thing behind them. Its shriek was terrifying. He shivered thinking about the way it smiled at them. The creature's hanging jaw was covered in rot and fungus. It had served as an undeniable reason to not stop.

"I hope it works. Or exhaustion will get the best of us." He took a swig of water.

"How did it get so fast? It was slow when we first saw it." "Magic makes it stronger. That is obvious. The thing probably fed on more magic and is looking for its next meal. We probably look like choice cuts of beef."

Anwar shuddered thinking of how something like that would feed on someone.

"So water? Are you one hundred percent sure it'll work?"

He tried to hide the worry in his voice and was disappointed he hadn't hidden it better. The places where his face was exposed were red from the cold.

"I ... can't be ... well, it worked with the other thing and nothing else has, so it's the best bet."

Anwar wasn't comforted by the answer, but he didn't have anything better to offer. If it had been that simple, they would have had no problem getting rid of their unwelcome guest.

"Would be a bad time if the water was frozen."

Elric's mouth drooped.

"I hadn't thought of that."

Anwar bit his lip harder than he meant to.

He snuck a glance behind them and saw the fast moving shape. Even from a quick look and how far away they were, he could see

it moving unnaturally. A new layer of goosebumps rose on his arms."How far away is it?"

Anwar urged his horse to go faster.

"Closer than I'd like. I didn't see it earlier today. He's almost on us." Elric leaned forward on Brolin.

They reached the embankment that lowered down into a roaring river. The rocks shuffled under them as they descended.

"That's a relief."

Small patches of ice dotted the shore. It wasn't enough to stop the torrent.

The water in places was crystal clear, with sparkling rocks lining the bottom. The river was deep, like an open mouth waiting to swallow whatever got too close, perhaps lured in by its beautiful appearance.

"Up there," Anwar pointed to a calmer portion of water.

The horses whinnied their protests.

Anwar glanced over his shoulder again. Nothing. He ushered Melina forward. She snorted but sloshed forward as the cold water beat against her lean muscle. He encouraged her forward, whispering and scratching her ear.

Elric followed behind them not quite a shoulder's length.

A terrible screech echoed on the shore.

They looked at each other, wide-eyed.

"Go," Elric mouthed.

The water deepened as the ground dipped. The splash on their clothes was numbing.

Rocks scratching against each other made them turn their heads.

Anwar could feel his neck become prickly.

"Why didn't you help me?" it asked in a whisper just above the noise of the river.

The slack-jawed creature gurgled and moved its jaw up and down.

They kept their eyes on it as they reached the opposite side.

It had changed a lot in such a short time. Where there were once two arms and legs there were now eight limbs altogether -- four on each side. The dark fungus holding it together gleamed and shone, with strange movements under its peeling skin. Long talon-like claws hungrily grabbed at small stones on the bank. It ground its elongated teeth together impatiently.

"What if it can jump?"

Elric studied it.

"If it could I think it would have by now."

"Help me," it pleaded.

Anwar drew his dagger.

Elric looked transfixed as it paced back and forth.

The creature tested the water with a talon. It squealed as skin burned from its finger. A low growl sent a warning to them.

"I ... AM ... HUNGRY."

"Elric?" he asked without looking at him.

"Yes?"

"Could we use magic to drown it?"

The creature tested the water with another howl.

"We need to get it into the water."

Elric summoned his magic. A line of larger rocks floated from the

shore around him into a line. He flicked his wrists and they rotated and formed an arching bridge towards the creature.

It stopped moving and tilted its head, watching intently. "Summon some of your magic halfway on the path," Elric said, breathing hard.

Anwar's eyes glowed a bright white. Sparks shot from his palm, forming a brilliant miniature sun. Tendrils of fire and heat moved around quickly like snakes. The creature's face contorted.

"Soooo hungry," it whispered.

The magic floated forward onto the middle platform.

A rut-like laughter erupted from it. It clawed onto the first rock with hesitation.

An eerie smile twisted its face. The white light of the magic casting shadows on its face didn't help. It coughed as it drew closer and closer to the orb.

"Just a little more," Elric said, now drenched from strain. The creature reached out to the orb with jittery fingers.

"Now!" he yelled.

The orb disappeared and the rocks crumbled under its feet. The creature gasped and grabbed wildly in all directions. A feral yell echoed. It tumbled head first into the water. Its scream nearly made them deaf. Its skin peeled away in large pieces as white bone came out from underneath

the growth. The black fungus disintegrated and a clean skeleton remained. It tumbled into pieces where once muscle and ligaments had held it together and was pulled downstream.

The water was dark for only a moment before turning back to crystal clear as before.

Anwar let out a held breath.

"Water was a good idea."

Elric wiped his forehead of sweat and took in long breaths. "Sadly," he gulped, "There could be more of these things. We don't know how many there are."

Anwar shook his head and lent his shoulder to him.

"Are you alright?"

He took him under his grip.

"Holding those boulders up expended a lot of magic."

"I'll be alright," Elric waved, "Just rusty is all."

He helped him over to the horses and set him down against a large natural rock wall.

"I hope the Warlock knows more than we do. It's not like we could carry around water buckets everywhere."

"Not a bad idea," Elric said as he closed his eyes.

CHAPTER 8

The mountains were the source of the frigid air, like wraiths that silently awaited the beckoning call of those that were to eventually meet their fate. It was a place where mumbled legends and myths became reality. Pine and cedar trees stood erect, unaffected by the once buffeting snow that had fallen and turned into a layer of ice on the ground.

The horses trudged meticulously along, if not without some bit of anxiousness.

"How are we to know where the path is if it's covered up?" Elric motioned to the canopy and further beyond to the formations of mountains. Their regal silence was intimidating as they looked like jagged fingers. He pointed to the centermost one.

"Irregardless of the path, that is where we are to go. There is the hold of the Warlock."

The mountain flattened out on the other side of the jagged edge. "Kind of a bit over the top, don't you think?"

Elric's eyebrow raised.

"The best place to guard the realm, I suppose. None would come here for the pleasant climate and atmosphere," Anwar harrumphed.

"I don't know about you, but I'm already tired of all this ice. Maybe it's a good thing, though, because I doubt we will see any of those creatures then. I hope it works the same as water does."

"I don't fancy being chased, either."

The sun was almost bluish against the curling frigid air.

They took time to rest a good portion of the night below a tree that was wide and provided a shelter against anything that would come from above. They replenished themselves with scraps.

As they sat down, Anwar felt his muscles pull and ache. He could only imagine how Elric felt. He looked up and noticed a raven sitting perched in the tree. It cocked its head when he made eye contact with it. It cawed its displeasure and blinked its beady black eyes.

Elric noticed it, too. They didn't know what to make of it, so both of them sat still.

It tilted its head back and forth and cawed again. It hopped closer with its quick movements, pausing here and there to titter in place. Snowy powder fell from the branch that it moved around on.

"To think I'd be cautious of a bird," Anwar muttered.

Elric tilted his head, copying the bird's gesture.

The raven ruffled its feathers on its neck and more sprouted in plumes. The bird growled, tilted its head, and jumped to another branch, turning its head sideways to see if they were watching it. It fluttered its shiny black feathers. A heap of them fell into a pile, standing out starkly against the white snow. It took to the air and feathers fell behind it perfectly into a line. It growled and cawed as it flapped away. As he was nearly out of sight, the bird burst into a crimson light, showing to them now in detail the signs of the stone path.

"Ah," Anwar said, "So it was a raven that wasn't a raven." Elric scratched his nose, "Hmmm. Isn't that something ... well, what have we to do but follow it?"

They assembled the horses and mounted them, following along the stone. Anwar wasn't sure if it was a good idea to follow every magical

bird, but he was too tired to think. He also was happy to see the mirthful look on Elric's face as they rode onward.

The feathers curled around the uneven path and led to more hazardous rocks and small cliffs until they came to a faded stone staircase. Despite the drifting wind, the feathers held in place as if they were glued there. They followed the staircase. The feathers thinned out where it had "disappeared" and what they originally thought was a mountain was actually a giant man-made platform.

Nothing made much sense where magic was involved.

They moved through a ward without knowing it. The warm tingling sensation scared them both. The ward did not harm them.

"That was stupid of me," Anwar said, "Of course there would be wards."

"Don't worry. I don't think those are there to harm us. Only those who would cause harm."

They both stopped in place. Before noticing the ward, they had seen only empty space. Now, where there had been nothing, there was a black and marble structure. Ravens' wings curled outward onto the ground and a large open raven's mouth overlooked the courtyard. In the eyes were blinking purple flames and on its wings were lanterns of the same color that flickered with the wind. The hold itself was cut of fine rock and glass; the presence it gave made them realize that there were more magical traps throughout that they may need to be wary of. They dismounted their horses as the purple flames began to spin rhythmically with each of their steps. The horses reared back and ran into the far side of the hold.

"Where are they off to?" Anwar asked.

The ringing noise in the air seemed to beckon the horses away.

Elric shrugged, "That's the least of our worries. We are now stuck here until the Warlock wants us to leave -- unless he doesn't. The horses will be fine. Or they won't."

Anwar didn't like the cryptic nature of it at all. They walked past statues of wizards with unseeable faces behind hoods. Each was representative of the sect of the order of mages. He recognized his own in the shape of the owl. He turned up his nose at seeing the symbol of the scourge mages with their vulture.

The others among them were various animals representative of all wizards everywhere. Animals lined their cloaks. They each looked as if they were staring at their open palms.

The ground vibrated and in the hands of each statue purple fire ignited as they passed them.

They saw the rich brown door open slowly. Despite it being open to them, they couldn't see what was inside. Anwar kept pace with Elric, who seemed none too impressed with everything. He, however, could have explored the courtyard alone all day if he'd had the time.

They felt the same warm tingling sensation as they had in the ward when they passed through the door. The room was dark as the door continued to turn inward and then closed just as slowly behind them.

The chamber was full of torches and books. Sitting among them was a figure who didn't notice them, reading a fully extended scroll. The figure was of a medium height. On one shoulder pad was the owl and on the other was the raven. Both sides had an arrangement of feathers of white and black. The cloak was of fine dark purple with archaic symbols lining it, representative of the rule of the Warlock in the realm. His face was ashen brown. His eyes were light gray and his hair was short and silver. His jaw was angular and he looked to be younger than Elric but older than Anwar.

He looked up slowly. The intensity of his gaze made them stop in place.

"Anwar Brighteyes, Elric Shatterblade, it is a pleasure." His deep voice boomed like thunder.

Elric and Anwar bowed as was customary.

Anwar had never met him before, but he knew his name. He simply explained it away to himself as magic.

The Warlock motioned to finely clothed seats adjacent to him. They obliged.

"One of you smells of lavender."

Anwar tried not to look at Elric.

"That is strange since you come from the south."

Elric nodded, "There's an important reason we have come to see you."

The Warlock folded his arms. Their leader of mages was only accessible if the magic of the warlocks wards deemed it worthy of his time. For them to gain access meant to him it must be.

Elric withdrew the two vials and put them on the corner of the table. The Warlock unfolded his arms. He leaned forward.

"Now what would you be doing with plague powder?" His massive hand gingerly picked up the powder and he held it in his palm.

"This hasn't been seen since even before my lifetime. Yet here it is …" he looked up, "why?"

Anwar cleared his throat.

"I was sent by Ulrith to investigate a strange sickness among the witch wood …."

He explained what he had discovered and how he had met up with Elric for help. Elric relayed his side of the story up until the moment they arrived at the hold. Before they knew it, it felt like hours had passed by. The Warlock put a knuckle to his mouth as he listened with full attention. As they finished, a dark shadow fell over his face.

"We came to you because Elric thought you would know what needed to be done to stop this new plague." Elric placed the book beside the vials.

The Warlock stood up and picked up the residue of the creature. "Someone has successfully created themselves a Plague Soul."

He looked at them both.

"What is that?" Elric asked uncharacteristically.

The Warlock straightened his robe.

"A Plague Soul. A shell of a monster that feeds on magic. So much so is its hunger that it kills and transforms any that it bleeds dry. A scourge to this world, and not of this world."

"A Plague Soul …" Elric tested the word, "I have never heard of a thing like that."

The Warlock grinned sullenly.

"As you shouldn't. The councils back then decided to burn any writings of them. Any knowledge of them. Which was a mistake. You cannot erase something, no not completely by not telling its story. The Plague

Souls are the reason we have instituted the Raven Doctors. It sounds like this Plague Soul has surpassed even their magic." He turned to them.

"But you've helped tremendously. Water is the key. If not for that knowledge I don't know where we'd be."

Elric tilted his head, "You mean you haven't had word of any others?"

The Warlock shook his head.

"There has been no word given to me. I sensed a plague but that's what the raven doctor sect is for. This ... this requires my attention.

Whatever did it did so under my watchful eye. How, without arousing my suspicion, I don't even know."

"Could you contact Urlith? She was the one who asked me to investigate the sicknesses."

The Warlock nodded and rolled up his sleeves. He removed a small mirror from a shelf and placed it in the center of the room. He waved his hand over it. It shook and sparked. The face of the mirror turned dark. He waved his hand over the mirror again. Still darkness.

Anwar knew what that meant without having to ask. Ulrith would have to

be dead for that to happen.

He looked dismayed.

"I fear the worst."

He rubbed his forehead.

"Let's try the archives."

He waved over the mirror. A dark room came into view. The archive was viewable by any wizard if deemed to have pure intentions. Books were scattered on the floor. There were blood stains.

“We were there not short of a week ago!” Elric said.

“The bodies are gone,” Anwar said in a whisper.

The Warlock waved his hand over the mirror. The reflection returned. “I must head to the archives and secure any unprotected books and scrolls. If a Plague Soul got in, the very magical protections may cease to exist.”

“We will go with you,” Anwar said, “if it isn’t too much trouble.” The Warlock considered it a moment and nodded.

“My magic should be able to carry all three of us. Anything beyond that would be a problem.”

Elric agreed.

The Warlock grinned crookedly as he rolled up his sleeves. “I hope you don’t get nauseous easily.”

Purple smoke rose at their feet and pulled them into a vortex of powerful magic. Anwar felt like he was going to be sick.

CHAPTER 9

The world spun as they exited the hazy cloud of magic that boomed and made the air vibrate. Anwar fell headlong over a stack of dusty books. Elric and the Warlock stepped out of it like mist on a summer's morning.

Anwar picked himself up awkwardly. He dusted off his robe. "The first time always gives you motion sickness and clumsiness," the Warlock said, extending his hand.

He took it and noticed Elric rummaging through papers.

The once radiant tower had been completely decimated. Pages were torn to shreds or drenched in red and black. The once vibrant colors were dull and lifeless. There was only the quiet. Elric sighed as he tossed papers away.

"All of it lost …"

The Warlock nodded, "To think how many wizards might be lost to us now," he pushed a pile of paper with his foot.

They tumbled to the floor, scattering and covering empty spaces. "You said the Plague Soul stayed inside until it had wizards to chase, correct?"

"Yes," Elric said, "We believed it to have to do with the weather, seeing as any and all water killed it."

The Warlock walked to the door to the exit of the archive, propping it open with his hand.

The beginning of a torrential downpour of rain brought noise into the library. A crackle of lightning from a storm thundered. He closed the door.

“There may be some here still,” he whispered. “I need you to look for any survivors. Or anything out of the ordinary, but quietly and no magic, of course.”

“Didn’t we just use magic to get us here?”

“Yes, but that’s not an issue. It was used to get us here and ceased the moment we arrived.”

“Ah.”

Anwar shrugged, “Well, from the noise, if there were any here, they would have come out by now.”

“Or drew closer,” Elric said. “We still need to be careful. I can light a torch to aid in our search.”

The Warlock agreed, “If you should run into trouble, head back to the bottom floor.” He gestured to the door, “I’m going to search the grounds for any signs of who is the root cause of this.” He pulled his dark purple hood over his head.

“Be careful ...”

He paused, “... and don’t die, of course.” He closed the door behind him.

“Not my exact impression of what meeting the Warlock would be like,” Anwar grumbled.

Elric grabbed one of the torches from the wall and lit it with a spark of flint.

The warmth was welcome on the desolate scene. The flow of the flames rippled across the dark walls.

"To think we could have met the same fate had we stayed …."

"If not for you, I would have been … thank you," he said awkwardly.

"It was just a coincidence. I know you would have gotten out.

You're wise; that's the reason I came to see you."

Anwar picked up a book that was intact. He turned it over and nearly laughed.

Spells and How to Spell Them.

He tossed it aside.

They looked around on the first floor, sifting through anything that looked interesting, but found nothing. The blood had long dried and whoever had been there hadn't been there in a long time.

They followed the staircase. The many floors looked one and the same. Books were tarnished and had burn marks where it looked that some of the wizards had tried to fight back against the monsters.

Scratch and bite marks accompanied by an indicative color were further clues as to what had occurred. There were strangely no bodies.

"It's crazy to think that they *all* turned."

Elric agreed.

"That's unlikely. For a hold of wizards to fall means there was more to it than that. As inept as most of them were, they weren't only capable of mere card tricks."

He was holding another book and tossed it to the ground.

Anwar dusted off his hands after rummaging through a stack of scrolls.

“This is a murder scene with little to no evidence,” Elric said. “Can we examine the blood?”

Elric shook his head, “This blood is tainted. Dried with nothing to examine almost as though ...”

“... someone muddled it,” Anwar finished.

Elric slowly shook his head. He could tell that the old man’s gears were turning trying to figure this riddle out.

Anwar looked closely at the liquid. It didn’t look like blood anymore. It was hard to the touch, and seemed like paint.

“What could they have done?”

Elric shrugged.

“They could have removed the life component from the blood. Making it untraceable. Thus the reason the blood looks strange.” Anwar turned away from the wall.

“How much magic would be needed to determine that?”

Elric looked thoughtful.

“Near to none. It would be safe to use.”

Anwar nodded, “Do you know the spell?”

Elric looked exhilarated, “In my potion making I’ve learned a few to assist me.”

He let his hand hover over the stain. He muttered words quietly. He squinted his eyes shut.

After a moment, he took a step back. He bit his lower lip.

Anwar gave him a questioning look when he didn’t speak immediately.

“There is nothing,” he said finally.

"Nothing?"

Elric looked bewildered.

"Nothing."

He put his hand over it again. He seemed dissatisfied.

"There's no anything. No components. No life, no magic, nothing to tell us anything."

He looked at the stain with interest.

"It's as if there isn't anything here at all. Not even the color of the stain. It's unbelievable."

An eerie realization came over him.

"They don't just take magic. They feed on everything entirely,"

Anwar confirmed.

Elric looked saddened.

"No trace of who they were."

Anwar felt a knot in his stomach. To be killed was one thing, but to have one's complete existence erased was another, more terrifying concept.

"These things are worse than we thought."

Elric rubbed his beard.

"We need to get out of here."

A thud made them both jump. They made eye contact. Thunder rumbled loudly.

They both let out a breath.

"The Warlock needs to know this. It could be vital to classify what or who would do this."

The sound of the storm grew more and more intense by the moment. The rafters and supports shook more fiercely as the rain pounded down harder.

"Should we try to save any of the books?"

Elric shook his head, "The Warlock has people who will do that for him. If there is anything salvageable, that is."

He looked at another book and snorted. Only paltry and insignificant.

As they had been going through the tower, he had hardly found anything worth salvaging.

Lightning struck outside of the window; the sky was dark. The brief strike let an all encompassing light shoot through the archive. Anwar froze as it went back to dark. The light had flashed the image into his vision and he could see it even though it was now dark again. He didn't look directly at what he saw for fear that whatever or whoever it was would make themselves known.

"Elric," he whispered, "Get over there."

He pointed to a still standing shelf that had some books remaining on it, at least enough that they could get behind.

They stood behind the shelf and Anwar kept peering around it to make sure nothing was approaching. He felt like something was right behind him at all moments.

"I saw something," Anwar said.

The torch they had been carrying had allowed them to only see small portions of the room, but now he could see for sure what would have been their death if not for the convenience of the light.

“There’s someone or something over there.” He didn’t point but moved his eyes.

“I don’t know what it is, but all I saw was a dark shape that had hands and feet.”

Elric nodded, “Get out your dagger. We don’t know if it’s a creature or someone that stayed behind. Since they haven’t made themselves known, we can only assume it or they have malevolent intentions.”

Anwar wordlessly drew the dagger and held it up against his leg, out of view.

Elric peered around the bookcase.

“However, us moving over here may make them suspicious.” They both took breaths. Neither of them felt like they could draw in enough breath because their chests were tight from the unease.

They were quiet as they hunkered down. They could almost hear the quiet but knowable sound of something breathing in and out. It was light and soft, unlike the Plague Soul that had been chasing them. It did not seem to be bound to the insatiable hunger that the soul was. It was likely human.

They both seemed to wordlessly say it to each other.

A single piece of paper shifted below the figure’s foot.

Anwar eyed the place he had heard it come from through a space in the books. The storm rumbled. Lightning flashed again.

He felt his breath catch in his throat and chills go throughout his whole body.

Whoever or whatever it was had moved closer. They were tall and lanky and had a dagger at their side. The cloak wasn’t just black -- it was all encompassing darkness. It created a void around them when they moved. Likely a result of some sort of magic. He blinked his eyes as the image faded away from him.

"Throw the torch," Anwar mouthed and pointed, "There."

Elric tossed it to where he had motioned. The torch clattered onto the floor and caught some of the books on fire in embers and small flames.

They both gasped upon the realization.

The thing was not a person. It had no skin or muscle; it was all bone. The bones were yellowed and disgusting looking with globs of black fungus clinging to them in strings. It screamed. A nightmarish noise.

A Plague Soul.

He now realized that the cloak wasn't a cloak at all but rather the plague fungus providing a covering for it.

Anwar stood his ground as it walked quietly around the flames. It waved its boney fingers and the flames extinguished. The dark returned. It clamped its teeth together with clicking noises.

They backed slowly to another pile of books as it reached blindly around the shelf. They held their breath as its fingers grabbed air. Elric covered his mouth as the creature made a low growl. It pulled the shelf as if it weighed nothing and slung it against the wall in a crash of leather and paper.

They hunkered down lower as they crawled along the ground quietly.

The monster took in a deep breath and stood still. They could barely make it out from around the pile. The storm was loud, which they knew unfortunately meant the Warlock would not have heard the crash. Anwar let out a breath and brandished the dagger. He moved around the other side of the pile with his eyes fixed on the still form of the creature. It breathed in and out in shallow breaths with only its chest moving. Its long fingers were limp next to it. He couldn't make out any other details as he crouched and readied the dagger.

Elric watched with his breath in his throat.

Anwar readied himself as the storm rumbled. The thunder flash was enough light as he leapt and drove the dagger into the chest of the figure.

He felt bone against the blade and he let go of it as it dug into its chest. He gasped as the creature seemed unaffected and the dagger clanked to the floor. He realized his mistake as he had ripped its cloak, revealing the same yellowed bones.

Its head popped and slowly turned up. Its smile was crooked and bright yellow eyes met his gaze. It groaned as both of its hands swept at him from either side.

Anwar dropped to the ground, retrieved the dagger, and swiped at its arm. He felt the contact but there was no sign of it having done anything to the creature. Elric rose from the book shelf, electricity surrounding his arms.

The creature turned hungrily to the old wizard. It whispered something under its breath as it threw Anwar out of the way. He crashed into books. He held his back as he laid sprawled out.

He could only watch as the creature lumbered forward, moving closer and closer to its next meal.

CHAPTER 10

Anwar groaned as his vision fluttered. He tried quickly to regain his breath as it had been knocked out of him.

Elric's arms shook from the powerful arcs of lightning that burned the floor.

The creature cackled as he reached out to touch the magic. Elric's eyes illuminated for a split second and the charge of magic shot from him in a rumble like the storm outside. The streaks of electricity struck the creature in the chest and sent it hurdling backwards. It soared through the room and crashed headlong into the wall. The wall shattered, opening a hole that sent it straight through from the pure force.

The creature tumbled into the rain. Elric strode forward as the creature squealed uncharacteristically. The cloak it wore disintegrated and the fungus burned away. It pulled at its coating and fell to the ground as more and more water rained down on it. Now it was a mere skeleton, naked to the storm. It was dead.

Elric kicked it with his foot and the bones fell apart. Anwar clumsily made his way over to him. They were both drenched and couldn't hear because of the downpour.

Elric fell to his knees as Anwar caught him before he hurt himself. "You are full of surprises, old man," Anwar jested, putting his arm under his shoulder.

Elric laughed.

"That was reckless, even for you."

Elric shrugged, "I figured if I hit it hard enough I could force it into the rain, and …" he nodded to the pile of bones, "… I was right."

Anwar gave him a grateful laugh through the storm.

He helped him walk back to the shelter of the archives. They stepped through the almost man-shaped hole in the wall. The archives were as dark as they had been before, but the light from the storm enabled them to see better.

The Warlock greeted them with fiery purple eyes and ignited palms.

"What happened?" he exclaimed.

Anwar leaned Elric against the wall out of the weather. "A Plague Soul, Elric saved me by blasting it into the rain."

The Warlock's magic didn't extinguish. It was only then that he noticed the fresh blood on his brow.

"What happened to you?" Anwar asked.

The Warlock shook his head, "We need to leave. Immediately. There are mages here that I was only able to stun. There is also a lich among them."

"A lich?" Elric questioned with a shortness of breath.

"I saw its phylactery. The Plague Souls are doing its bidding." Anwar gave him a questioning look. There were several words in that statement that didn't make much sense to him.

A booming rumble shook the other side of the tower. They turned as the building shook. Small pieces of the main beams cracked and chips of stone clattered to the floor.

The Warlock rushed them and summoned the swirling magic around them. Anwar wasn't able to prepare as the room started to spin and rotate. His vision blurred. The journey was haphazard as he felt himself being jerked roughly, unlike the first time they had journeyed.

In a blink of an eye, they all lay sprawled out on a smooth marble floor.

Anwar coughed roughly but the nauseous feeling passed quickly.

He sat up too soon, though as his vision blacked out. He sat back again.

The Warlock was already on his feet.

"Both of you stay still. It will take some time before you can stand without fainting. I apologize for having to do that so abruptly, but it was worth it."

Elric didn't argue as he turned on his side.

"Where are we?"

The Warlock paced back and forth, rubbing his brow.

"My magic sealing room. A place where we cannot be followed." They both looked around and noticed how pristine it looked in comparison to the other room that they had been greeted in. It made no sense that something so large could exist in a hold so small. Magic was the only explanation. With that, fancier adornments were on the wall such as cloaks, staves, orbs, books and other mysterious artifacts.

Anwar tested his footing and slowly stood, extending a hand to

Elric.

"You saw a lich?"

The Warlock had a troubled look on his face.

"Yes. Along with four other wizards."

Elric dusted himself off.

"You actually saw a phylactery?"

He nodded and waved his hand.

"At first I thought it was a raven doctor. This one, however, was unlike any one I had ever seen. It wore a mask with six eyes in total and they glowed a bright green. When I got closer, I saw the tube-like phylactery, and it was pouring something into it, which glowed red. It was standing over a body. The wizards around it attacked me, whom I recognized to be scourge mages." He made a fist, "I held them at bay as the lich lifted its bony fingers and nearly killed me with a bolt of raven fire. Luckily, your magic distracted him enough to miss a lethal blow. I cast a blinding light spell and ran to you."

Anwar shook his head, " A lich? Of all things ... I didn't think those even existed."

"They were always thought to be legends," Elric added. "Lichs are known to feed on the lifeforce of the living in order to gain immortality. The means have been unknown."

"Until now," Anwar said, "the Plague Souls ...."

The Warlock nodded, "Along with many other books that thought the same. Though they suggested it was possible, up until this point no reasonable thought was given to whether they could actually be made. Now though, we are dealing with one. I am sure of it."

Elric cleared his throat.

"We discovered in the tower by examination of the blood of the victims through means of a splinter spell that there was no lifeforce or any indication of life. The Plague Souls take everything including magic from its meal."

The Warlock's eyes widened, "It makes sense then. The lich must use those creatures to fuel its only lifeforce. Considering a lich is undead."

"So steal life from others to fuel your own?" Anwar shook his head, "Leeches serve more benefit than that."

"Can any more of them be made?" Elric asked.

The Warlock pressed his fingers to his temple.

"In theory, yes. If one exists now, then it is possible. I need to send a message to all the Warlocks and even a message to the Archmage. This may be even beyond me."

Anwar thought about the hierarchy of the magical world: those like Elric and Anwar served at the bottom level; then there were gilded, like Ulrith who managed specific casters; warlocks who ruled regions; and then the supreme authority of magic was the Archmage.

The Warlock lifted a finger to his temple and touched it to the small mirror that seemed to come from thin air. He muttered under his breath for a few minutes. They both watched him like he was something in a holding tank.

"It is done. They need only read the message. For now, I need your help."

Anwar nodded, his brown eyes brightened.

"What do you need of us?"

The Warlock moved his fingers around in thought.

"The village of Grayhill is close to the archives, and the next location they will likely target. I am only guessing since it is the largest known populace near the archive and falls under its protection. With there being a void where that power used to be, I must step into it. We need to stand between the people and the lich."

He looked at them with his intense yellow eyes aflame with purpose.

"I informed the warlocks and Archmage that we would make a stand there. I cannot guarantee we will be successful or that we will live past the encounter. I am calling on both of your oaths to fulfill what needs to be done to protect my people, our people. With none of our wizards at the hold, I fear we will be heavily outnumbered."

"We are both willing," Elric said, "But my magic isn't as powerful as it used to be; I may be a liability to us."

Anwar gave him a sidelong look as he recalled the lightning, and the floating rocks.

The Warlock smiled, "I highly doubt that." He adjusted his hood.

"First things first, you are promoted to the title of Gilded. As for your magic, I have some weapons not unlike what I'm wearing that will be at your disposal."

He motioned to the fabric. Though the majority of it was purple and black, the archaic symbols illuminated.

"These are heavily enchanted. The magic will respond to you according to your latent ability. The symbols will glow when you find the appropriate weapon."

He shifted his weight.

"I will leave you two to be tested by my magic." He turned to them, "Think of any weapon you would like and merely state it; otherwise, check this room. You can find most anything here. I will return within the hour to gather you for Grayhill."

His eyes glowed as he turned one last time.

"If you decide between now and then that you do not want to come, I will not hold it against you."

CHAPTER 11

Smoke. Greenish haze surrounded the plains to the south of Grayhill. The sky was darkened, yet the smoke itself seemed to carry a strange illumination due to the lack of sunlight. The storm that had been above the archives had left, but tumultuous clouds lingered overhead. The gray and green light cast an eerie foreshadowing. The damp ground smelled rich and earthy.

The men and women who could not fight had been ordered into their houses, to bolt the doors in preparation for what was coming. Grayhill was a peaceful city. The archive had always been a superior deterrent in the past. That time was no more. The strength of the city came to the forefront, as one unequivocally unprepared for an engagement such as this. The most anyone could muster was a pitchfork or rarely even a dull dagger.

Anwar walked along the guard tower on the southeast side of the city. He observed the green gas with fascination.

"What do you make of it?" he asked Elric.

Anwar fumbled with the light bearing clothes given to him by the Warlock. It was a type of cloak that was meant to enhance spellcasters of his ability, and specifically only beneficial to a light wizard. The cloth was yellow and gold. The ancient symbol of a hand bearing a flame rested in its center with a long forgotten language bannered around his sleeves and hems. Embedded into the material's center was a gold gem.

Elric wore his usual garb but wielded a black staff with a teardrop stone at its top. It glowed like a miniature white sun. When the Warlock first saw him with it, Elric saw a strange smile creep onto the Warlock's face. Elric didn't know what the staff was, only that it responded to his magic.

"Green normally means poison. Though in a lich's hands, who knows what it'll do," he said, scratching his thumb on the surface of the staff.

Raven Doctors stood silently below them. Their birdlike movements were almost unworldly as they stood watching the smoke. They were the only form of magic wielders in Grayhill and had silently agreed to assist the Warlock. They leaned vicariously on their staves, watching much like an owl would a rat. Their tattered black cloaks moved with the light breeze. Any sound made them turn and peer at it with tilted heads.

The city bell churned and tolled. Each loud ring echoed between the alley ways.

The grates surrounding the city were full of flowing water. The underground plumbing system that the city employed provided a fortuitous opportunity to use against any Plague Soul that happened to wander too close to the city. They had seen none and were beginning to wonder why the lich had made no move on the city. They had been waiting for several hours. Tense, anxious waiting.

Anwar took a long drink of wine from a wineskin.

Elric tapped his staff on the floor and opened the small book that he had carried with him. He had done this repetitively every so often. He claimed he wanted to be sure there was nothing that they missed in regards to the plague powder. It could have been just nerves that made him do it, but Anwar didn't mind. He only wished that he could divert his eyes from the plains. He was afraid that if he did that, he, too, would miss something important.

The Warlock was at work procuring more barrels of water and liquid to use if needed. He had not been seen within the city ever since they had teleported. He had given them one clear directive: Guard the city. Do not let any of them inside. At all costs.

Anwar reached his hand down to the newly added dagger. It was white, with the inscription of a lone dragon grasping the hilt. It had fallen unceremoniously from its position on the wall in the Warlock's hold and would not, despite his actions, return to its place. Elric told Anwar that it was magic that had made it fall and to not put it back. As much as a dagger was suited to him, he didn't really like the feel of it in his hands. It was as if it were made for someone else.

It felt odd. The dagger he had recently lost had been something he had carved through magic. It felt personal.

A screech owl broke the silence of the fog. It glided past the tower and nestled itself on a ledge. It darted back and forth, snatching moths that were drawn to their lights. He was distracted by it as it ruffled up and turned its head in an owl's natural way.

He looked up and saw a lone figure amongst the green fog. How he had missed it he didn't know. He nudged Elric, who was muttering to himself. He looked to where Anwar pointed. He closed the book and tucked it away.

His mouth was agape as he leaned on his staff.

The figure moved. Its hand extended out. As if it were … "He's pointing at us," Elric said. Anwar hooked his thumb on his belt.

As if from nowhere, black shapes began to move jerkily beside the figure.

He knew what they were based on the sporadic movements.

"Plague Souls," Anwar said.

He shook as he leaned on the ledge.

"Hundreds."

Elric scowled, "So many wizards lost."

Anwar noted that here and there were normal moving blotches. He squinted to make out the familiar symbol of the scourge wizards.

"This will be a war," he whispered.

Elric illuminated his staff and waved it back and forth -- the predetermined signal.

A whistle screeched below. A woman cried out as she stumbled over her own feet. The whistle had startled her as she was moving supplies.

He looked back to the horizon. The basins of water were positioned and hidden along the barrier of the wall. If that failed, then the plague would sweep through them, devouring all magic. This would provide the lich with the numbers to go uncontested.

More and more dark figures began to appear from the denseness of the fog, almost as if they were some joined entity.

"We will join them if we aren't careful," Elric leaned forward, looking. Anwar agreed and he made sure his supplies were tied tightly to him.

"Let's hope not."

CHAPTER 12

The sizable invasionary force halted into formation like a scattered wall. They surrounded them from all sides and stood waiting. Unrecognizable whispers drifted on the wind. The glowing-eyed lich stepped to the forefront.

He wore a leathery black beaked mask. Much like the raven doctors' but more sinister. It was trimmed in fine gold and an aura of green glowed from three eyes on both sides of the mask. The hood and that draped over it was pitch as night. Sinister and unknowable items were fastened to its side and shoulders. The shoulder pads were pointed and appeared to be made of stained bone. The triangular shape of tied bones gilded behind its head. The distinct glow of the metallic-glass vial on its side glowed a liquidy red.

The phylactery.

The lich halted as everyone stood tensely.

It tilted its head and turned slowly, taking them all in.

A skeletal finger pointed at the two of them in the tower. A chill went through Anwar's spine.

A sound of an explosion made him freeze in place. Out of the corner of his eye he saw the water spray into the sky.

He knew now what he had heard.

The wall below exploded in green fiery smoke. The wall containing all of the water churned and buffeted the houses below in a giant wave of force.

He watched helplessly as the soldiers below were swept away and slammed into the walls of structures that held against the water.

The tower creaked and moved. A sound of an almost groan.

Elric stamped his feet and staff.

"How did he ...?" He shook his head, clenching his teeth.

Anwar shook his head.

The water was all that they had to be able to stop the creatures. The lich withdrew his extended finger and let his arm droop beside him.

Although Anwar couldn't see it, he could almost feel its grin beneath its mask.

"What now?" Anwar whispered.

The water level began to lower.

"But everything is wet now, couldn't it still be manipulated?" He gestured to the damp ground of mud as the level steadily dropped.

Elric nodded, "You're right."

The green smoke surrounding the small army thickened. The lich didn't move. The smoke moved forward at a snail's pace.

Elric leaned forward.

The men below had recovered for the most part. The worst among them was a bruised shoulder. They moved back to their posts with murmurs.

The smoke was a thick wall of motion as it edged still closer. Anwar felt a bead of sweat trickle from his forehead. He wiped it with the back of his hand.

Elric shifted uncomfortably.

The room became musty and dry.

Anwar rolled up his sleeves. The heat was unbearable.

He looked down as warriors' faces were bleached red and sweaty.

Each of their faces gleamed.

Even the raven doctors seemed uncomfortable.

Anwar gave Elric a look.

"That isn't a poison spell …."

"It's meant to dry up the water."

Elric noted that the cloud had cleared half the distance.

"What do we do?" Anwar asked.

Elric closed his eyes and re-opened them.

"I can only do this once. You will have to protect me from here forward, seeing as I will only be able to cast minor defenses."

Anwar bit the inside of his cheek as he felt his wards shatter and the all encompassing spell of the enemy. He felt a jolt as his defense was tossed aside like a dirty cloth.

"What are you going to do?"

Elric lifted the staff in front of him.

The crystal glowed white. He lifted his opposite hand. A whistle carried through the air. Movement caught his eye and he saw the flapping flag. The wind had increased exponentially. He turned back to Elric who was deep in concentration.

The whistle was a roar as the flag barely hung onto its post. The green smog stopped its movement in the face of the wind. Those below stirred nervously.

Elric's forehead was rippled with lines as he snarled at the release of magic. Black clouds encircled overhead. The warm air was replaced by cold. The wind formed into a ripping force that tore through the green wall, tossing it away. The collision sounded like thunder. The gas swirled around at the center of the typhoon until it faded with the wind. The spiral of wind broke into smaller gusts until there was no more wind. The clouds disappeared as quickly as they had come.

Elric fell backwards as he released the magic. Anwar caught him under the arm.

Elric breathed roughly, his robe drenched in sweat.

"Th-that should suffice."

Anwar didn't want to say that Elric may have dried up most of the water in the process, but he was surely thinking about it. He was more than anything astounded that the old wizard had said he didn't have "much" magic and yet he was able to summon a wind storm.

"That was impressive old man."

Elric laughed with little air.

He leaned him on the edge.

The creatures overhead stirred angrily. The lich was unmoving except for its head which was tilted to the side.

"You stopped his spell."

Elric swallowed dryly and coughed.

"Let's hope so."

He reached into his cloak and handed him a skin of water. The men below stood at the ready. They seemed to be more confident to see a wizard on their side cast such a powerful piece of magic.

The lich straightened, pointed at the tower, and slowly dropped his hand.

The creatures screeched and charged towards them, their movements jerky and inhuman.

This could end in a massacre.

CHAPTER 13

The air was stagnant. Anwar allowed his magic to flow through him in preparation for what was coming. It wasn't just power that pushed him; it was the boiling of his blood that came in association with magic. The dagger felt rigid under his white knuckled grip. He moved it around nervously.

The black figures of the creatures were blurs as they tore across the land towards the walls. Their claws ripped into the muddy ground. The archers prepared their special arrows and notched them onto their strings.

It was amazing what glass could be melded into. They had hastily created glass orbs filled with water that once shot would break on contact. The glass was incredibly thin, and a local merchant had been using them for administering medicine. If not for Elric's quick thinking, they would not have been able to use them. The old wizard steadily carried his weight in gold.

Beforehand Elric had met with them and explained what the creatures were like. They would wait until they got close enough to hit the Plague Souls directly. He had also expressed to them that they were not to be underestimated, and yet not to be afraid of them.

The information was met with apprehensive looks, but eventually they came around due to how seriously it had been delivered to them. "I hope this is enough," Anwar said.

The world seemed suddenly to slow down. He felt his heart beat like miniature rumblings of thunder as the first Plague Soul ripped into the wall and powered upwards.

The first arrow released, followed by a shatter of glass and the sound of water. The creature's claw was struck and it lost its grip as it howled and tumbled to the ground. The creature squealed uncharacteristically and scraped downward.

Anwar summoned his magic. The orb of fire floated in place as he pushed it away with the flick of his wrist. Following behind it were red sparks. It halted in front of the wall, dead center. He held his hand in place to control it from going any further.

The creatures turned to it like ravenous wolves as he heard the murmuring of their whispers. It sounded like a hundred voices.

However, he caught one word in particular.

Hungry.

The archers looked pale-faced as they steadied their bows. Before them was a terrifying sight for anyone to see even if they had been warned.

One Plague Soul was almost upon the fire when Anwar moved it. A dozen arrows struck it in an explosion of water. Its body went limp and it fell like a ragdoll, toppling over others that were making the climb.

Anwar snuck a glance and noticed the lich was no longer out in the plains. He had disappeared.

"Elric, where did he go?" he said under the strain of his magic. Elric shook his head.

"I'm not sure. He just disappeared!"

Anwar looked around desperately.

"You had to have seen him do something?!" Another Plague Soul met its end by a projectile.

Elric shook his head. Something caught his eye just out of his sight.

A shiver went through him.

"What is it?" he asked, still holding his magic as arrows barraged the monsters.

He turned and his heart sank.

Black powder floated in the center of the village. It fell in heaps and sheets.

He swallowed as he watched the breeze spreading it throughout all those in the square.

He took a deep breath. He had no time or ability to summon enough magic to stop it.

"Get out of here!" he waved his free hand at the men and women below.

They stopped what they were doing and turned to look at him. "GET OUT OF HE-"

The square exploded in green fire and black powder.

He winced as he turned in time to avoid seeing those unprotected wiped from existence. The image of a man burned into his eyes when he closed them. The horror in his face chilled him. He forced himself to open his eyes to escape it.

He turned back, squinting. The powder was everywhere. The whole of everything was covered by it. The floor, the grounds, and all of the huts and buildings were nothing but black powder.

The lich appeared from the dark blanket of plague as if it had been deep water.

Its arms were outstretched as a wave of fire reached out, striking the buildings.

Anwar was toppled over by the jolt as Elric's shoulder made bone breaking contact with the wall. The ripple made a cracking noise all around them.

Black powder flew in every direction.

He put his hand over his face as he felt it flow through the air. He felt his heart stop as he saw the black powder hit Elric full in the face.

CHAPTER 14

"Elric!"

He groaned as he rolled over.

The old wizard's body shook.

Anwar stood up unsteadily. The tower was now leaning. A massive fissure split it down the middle. He kicked aside rubble as he reached out for him. The gap was twice as long as he was tall and he could see miniature fissures forming in waves.

He watched as Elric's staff started to slip from his grip. He tried to stop the staff from falling, but it toppled from Elric's grasp. It fell into the hole and ricocheted, shattering on the ground. A river of plague powder poured down into yet more darkened sand.

He shook his head as he noted that the lich was walking with one hand raised and the other on his phylactery.

No time.

Elric's eyelids flickered as his mouth was open agape.

"Elric, are you alright?" he whispered as he attempted to rouse him.

The old wizard slurred indistinguishable words as he gasped for breath. Tears brimmed the corners of his black stained eyes. He moved his shoulder and bit down on his teeth with a grunt. "Stay down," Anwar said as he could feel the knot in his stomach tightening.

Elric opened one eye as tears filmed it.

"The powd-"

Anwar shook his head, "Don't worry about that right now." His voice was more shaky than he had wanted it to be. "We just need to get out of here." He crouched beside him.

"I have to find a way to get you up."

"Whyyyyy wooooon't yoooooouuuuu heeeeeelp meeeee ...."

The interruption surprised them both.

A rough, wet cough echoed up to them.

Anwar had to stop himself from punching the ground.

It seemed that the lich now had replacements.

"My shoulder ..." Elric said as he tried to push himself up.

He stopped him.

"Let me see what I can do." He pulled back the robe from the wizard's shoulder.

He nearly fainted at what he saw.

The shoulder was disfigured, but he saw black blotches and black snakes for veins colored below the surface. Black boils were slowly spreading along his under arm.

He covered him back up.

Elric's face had begun to show black veins around his eyes. "Elric, what can I do?"

His face looked more ancient than it had ever.

"Push me to that wall," he cringed.

Anwar nodded and despite how much he knew it was going to hurt him, he helped him to the wall.

Elric's body shook and his skin felt like an inferno to the touch. Anwar swallowed back tears as he lowered him to a sitting position. The old wizard drooped in place, unable to completely hold himself there.

He reached to help him, but Elric waved him away with a lazy motion from his unscathed arm.

"You have to listen very carefully to me, Anwar." He nodded.

"You have to destroy the lich's phylactery. That is the only way to break the curse of the powder."

Anwar knelt close to him to be able to hear his whispering better. "How can you be sure when you didn't know before?" Elric took in a raspy breath.

"I wasn't sure at first. Though it occurred to me when he blew apart this place that he was using them in accordance with one another. The green gas ... it fuels it somehow ...." Anwar bit the inside of his lip.

"You're sure."

The old wizard shook his head.

"I can only guess ...."

"Will it save you?"

Elric didn't say anything; he looked uncertain.

A commotion down below interrupted him. He edged to the hole and peered down.

The raven doctors were making their stand against the lich. Flashes of green and black erupted around them. The Plague Souls were running towards them like feral dogs in anticipation of a meal.

The masks!

An explosion of green shook the tower.

“I’ll be back for you, Elric.”

The wizard jerked.

“You may not like what you find when you come back.”

Anwar’s eyes flashed.

“Don’t talk like that.”

He watched as half a dozen raven doctors were holding off the onslaught of the lich and the souls.

Where is that so-called Warlock?!

He noticed Elric’s robe had ripped on a sharp piece of wall. The fabric hung loosely. That gave him an idea.

He took it and wrapped it around his mouth, making sure that it was clean of any of the powder. After he was satisfied, he took one final look at the old wizard. He hoped this wasn’t the last he would see of his friend.

He jumped through the crack towards the green light.

CHAPTER 15

Green fire streaked forward, pushing back the black powder and revealing the already transforming corpses and skeletons of those recently deceased. The raven doctors' staves were all raised with streams of fire snaking off from them. The lich cackled an echoing laugh as it watched them with its tilted head, its bone-white fingers flickering.

Anwar landed with a loud crackle beside them.

It seemed they had forgotten about him as they gave him a quick quizzical look but continued with their magical barrage. The lich had backed away with his arms folded as the Plague Souls gathered closer and closer.

How was their magic holding the souls off?

Anwar drew the dagger from his side. He felt the familiar tingle of magic preparing to be released.

Should I dare to even use it?

His eyes illuminated without him being able to control it. The magic rippled through him like a torrential downpour of rain.

It was almost as though his magic had a mind of its own. Without thinking, he felt heat radiate from his daggerless arm. He raised three fingers with his free hand. White flames flew from them and formed into palm sized spheres. He parted his fingers as the flames flew in different directions.

He felt fire snake into the dagger he held.

He looked at it clenched in his fist, which was covered in white fire. The dagger glowed and began to extend. White flames shot outward into an elongated blade. Fire winged out from the sides forming a crossguard.

He moved the fiery sword around. The flames stayed constant and held the shape. The fire seemed to move through the air seamlessly. He felt electrical heat radiate from his cloak. It was only then that he knew it was glowing a ghostly white.

The lich unfolded its arms and leaned forward, peering. He could tell whatever was going on with him was a source of concern for it.

He moved to the raven doctors and stood next to them. All the while the sword burned hungrily, its flame reaching out like fingers. He felt an overwhelming mix of power and exhilaration.

He only wished his magic would work against the creatures. One doctor motioned to him. He looked to be holding an invisible sword, making a hacking motion.

Anwar felt the flames move in circles around his feet. He noted something else. The plague powder retreated away from each of his steps like scurrying bugs.

He couldn't help but smile as even a Plague Soul retreated at his approach.

He could feel the lich's disapproval with each step. He swung the rippling blade. It cut straight through the middle of the Plague Soul. It cried out despite being in two pieces and faded into powder and a yellowed skeleton.

The raven doctors fought the remaining souls as he walked uncontested to within fifteen paces of the lich.

It tilted its head like a plague doctor and put one hand over the glowing cylinder. It was then he noticed the green light was not just light. There were shapes and orbs that seemed to move around its inside.

The lich's skeletal fingers popped with each movement--a noise he had not heard until now because he stood so closely to it.

He meant to say something but his mouth was clenched. White fire darted from his right eye. A solar flare of magic. He could feel his jaw locked in place.

He looked around as the plague powder moved toward the lich like a black river.

He slammed his blade into the ground, severing the stream. The lich tilted its head. Its eyes glowed like liquid emeralds. Anwar watched the raven doctors incinerate another Plague Soul.

A thought occurred to him.

Magic was working, but why? It's working because ....

Anwar summoned more fire to surround him in a spiral of flame. *No matter. If it worked it worked. But where was the Warlock?* He dove forward, landing on his right foot and throwing a ball of fire toward the lich.

The lich lifted its skeletal hand and held the fire in place. The lich closed his hand, extinguishing the fire, but not before scowling as it singed the inside of the bone.

He could almost feel the surprise of the lich as he turned the singed bone towards him, confused.

He moved closer and closer. He had never felt a thrill quite like this. He moved with a strange new agility. The lich didn't seem to care to notice.

He clenched his teeth and he drew back for a finishing blow.

The sword bore down, its blade hungry for retribution--for revenge. Just as it would have connected with its neck, the lich ducked under it and opened handed him in the chest, knocking him backwards along with his breath.

Anwar watched wide-eyed as he seemed to fall back in slow motion. The lich's sleeve caught fire and he tore it off before it went up in flames. The skeletal arm was black as soot with streaks of white.

The lich's arm was surrounded by plague powder. It circled it and formed a protective layer, making it look like charcoal skin.

He flexed it as Anwar rolled into a broken building. Groaning, he picked himself back up. He moved to a crouch as he took long drawn out breaths to reestablish his breathing.

Looked around at the broken wood and stone, he saw three Plague Souls come through the opening his body had created.

He summoned his magic, anticipating their attack.

CHAPTER 16

The blade sank into the ground. The final Plague Soul fell into a heap of bones.

He walked through the opening and noticed the green gas had returned. He waved his free hand around him, pushing it away from his face.

He looked down the long alley. Rubble littered the space. He didn't even see the raven doctors anymore. Nor did he see any more of the plague powder.

He could barely see the broken tower in the distance.

I hope Elric is alright.

Best not to think about it.

It was easy to do as a peculiar noise caught his ears.

A strange gurgling noise came from around the corner of some houses.

He edged his way to the corner and peeked around.

Raven doctors lay everywhere. And in the center stood the lich. It was weaving a black string with each movement into one of the bodies. Its fingers were not unsimilar to someone sewing something. Anwar pulled his head back. He made three finger sized orbs of concentrated light at will. He was surprised at how potent they were. The air around them vibrated. He rounded the corner and sent the projectiles headlong at the lich.

The first one ripped through the air, making a shrill noise as it left a tear in the open space.

As the lich looked up, it ripped through the mask in a terrible burning sear.

The lich was facing downward from the jarring blow. It looked up and only then did he truly realize what a lich was. The mask was torn. Underneath was the yellowed skull of the lich. Two of its six eyes glowed with hatred.

Anwar threw the next one, this time targeting the phylactery. The orb missed but grazed the robed side. He flung the next one and ran closer to the lich, his sword raised. The lich was so preoccupied with it, it didn't anticipate how close he had gotten.

Anwar was quicker this time as the lich turned his full attention on him in a gaping jaw of surprise.

The sword ripped through the metal casing of the phylactery. It sparked and shattered now that the physical binding was gone. Flashes of red and purple scattered, sending the lich backwards to the ground. Anwar stood over him. He awaited the lich to burst into flame, or melt, or something.

It didn't happen. Instead, a grinding noise came from the lich. He lowered his sword. Was it laughing?

The lich held its side as its eyes narrowed in on him.

He froze as he heard something breathing with moisture in its breath.

He turned around.

The raven doctors' bodies stood upright. Their wounds that had dispatched them were now joined to each other by the black lining that he realized was plague powder.

He used that time to create something.

The powder pulled them together. They formed a massive heap as the powder shaped them in a cruel and nasty process. The shape floated, enlarged, and stepped down onto the ground again. It finalized its transformation into a monstrous creature with eyes as equally green as its creator's.

Its claws flexed as its long head formed its beaked mouth--the result of the raven masks. It opened its sword-like beak and hissed.

"Heeeeeelp meeeee."

Anwar felt his body go numb.

Its body shimmered. The veins and thick muscles flexed as it moved forward on its upright legs. It was like a man, but bulkier and more hunched. Its beak shined with a film of red as it leaned its weight on its front arms. Long sword-length claws protruded from the side of its forearms.

The creature's jaw rattled as a curdling growl cut from its sharp-mouthed beak. A pink film of skin on either side of its mouth stretched as it screeched.

Anwar stood his ground and firmly gripped the sword.

The lich behind the monster cackled as its teeth clattered together. It moved one finger across its throat symbolically. He noticed one of its green eyes was no longer green. The six eyes were now five.

He felt the realization hit him.

The lich had more phylacteries.

The lich moved into the shadows. He moved to chase him as the whistle of the creature's forearm blade nearly decapitated him.

He froze in place, unnerved.

"Donnnnn't leeeeeeave," it said in an eerily human voice.

Anwar willed his magic around his body and allowed it to focus into the sword. He felt the edge of the pull of his magical strength. Even still, he called it forward. The lich wouldn't escape.

He swung his magical rage at the bird monster. He felt the weight fall with his blade as it roared with intense fire. With all the momentum, the clawed blade caught the sword in mid-swing, completely halting it. The monster's eyes gleamed with excitement.

Anwar snarled as he could push no further.

The flames ran up the monster's arm. The monster made a yelping noise as it threw Anwar and the sword away from it.

It wiped at its arm, tearing flesh along with putting out the fire.

Anwar coughed as he hit the side of the building. He felt his head ringing and something wet on the side of his face. The mask tore away from his mouth.

He forced himself to his feet and he could feel his vision blurring.

The creature's arm showed bone where the fire had latched on. The bird monster's wound healed as more plague powder ran up its body and into the wound.

The fire surrounding Anwar began to diminish.

Not now!

He strained to hold onto the magic, but it burned away like oil in a lamp.

He took a step back and saw the sword turn back into the dagger.

The flames snuffed out.

He had enough magic for one more attack. He summoned an orb of compressed light into his open palm.

He felt sweat drip down from his pounding head. He wiped at his eyes as some of it streaked through his vision. It burned, but he had no other option but to keep looking; otherwise, he could lose his life.

The creature was fully healed as it flexed its arm and then leaned forward on both arms.

Anwar drew back his arm as he prepared to throw the last-ditch bit of magic he had.

The green beady eyes looked at him hungrily with each lumbering step.

He focused on the only thing he could think of.

Its temple.

He released the orb with a blast of power that made his arm go numb. He fell down hard from the amount of force behind it. His throwing arm hung limply beside him.

The orb hit the creature dead in the face in an explosion of light and fire.

Anwar's eyes were full of sunspots as he didn't close his eyes in time. He blinked quickly and moved to stand.

A realization came to him.

Where were the rest of the Plague Souls?

CHAPTER 17

He nearly cried out as his vision returned to him. The exposed skull of the bird creature lay open as its eyes still stared at him. A steady stream of powder poured into the side of its head, recovering the impact of his magic. The veins and the inner workings of the skull looked disgusting as they still pumped and moved.

He felt the blood leave his face as he clutched the dagger close to him. He took a few lazy movements backwards. Every bit of him felt heavy and weak. He could tell by the unnatural movement of his arm that it was broken. And here that thing was staring at him as if he were hot soup on a cold day.

Its mouth opened wide as it squealed with glee with each jerky step. Anwar moved to stab with the dagger, but his arm was too heavy. Each step it took made him realize the count down on his life had begun.

He closed his eyes as he could smell the decaying breath of the creature.

He felt its shadow envelop him. Then he felt its wet saliva fall on him. Its roar stopped abruptly. He was tense, and after gathering what courage was left, he peered out of his eyes.

Some liquid continued to drizzle down on him, but it wasn't coming from the creature. In fact, the creature was on the ground writhing.

It wasn't saliva. It was water.

Rain!

The creature's body was shriveled into a malnourished version of itself. It lay on the ground as it steadily grew smaller and smaller, the yellow bones underneath it showing. It shuddered at the torrential downpour.

He would have almost felt pity for the bird monster if not for the fact it meant to eat him.

"Anwar!"

He looked behind the dissolving creature.

The Warlock stooped down beside him. Anwar winced at both his own pain and the Warlock's dreadful appearance. The Warlock was covered in bruises and gashes and either his or something else's blood. The regal appearance of an impression the Warlock had made the first time upon meeting was far gone.

"Are you all right?"

Anwar nodded.

"And Elric?"

He could hardly find breath in him. He was frozen. In the midst of the fighting he had forgotten his friend.

He motioned with his head towards the tower and mouthed, "There."

The Warlock looked around quickly before he raised his palm to him.

"I can't have you laying around unprotected." A shining yellow orb illuminated from his hand, "Here, take this."

The orb shot into his chest. He cried out as it felt like what he imagined being struck by lightning would be like.

He felt his body feel weightless and the Warlock was putting a hand under his armpit to pick him up.

"I don't have much substance left in me. The battle against the lich has brought me closer to death than I had hoped."

His smile was pearly white except for blood from his lip. "I did manage to attach a tracking spell on him, though."

Anwar felt a surge of magic inside of him. He had the energy to move. However, his hurt arm continued to pound through him like a miniature heartbeat.

The Warlock looked at his arm and pointed.

"We'll get a healer to look at that."

He turned at the smoking remains of the bird creature. All that was left were pure white bones of several human-like corpses.

Three raven doctors.

Anwar was saddened and proud of the raven doctors. He made it up in his mind that they would receive a proper burial. They all would, he thought, as he saw the remains of Plague Souls scattered across the ground in pure white.

They approached the dilapidated tower. It moaned and groaned under the steady downpour.

The Warlock summoned his magic and lifted pieces of broken beams into place. One after the other rotated into the space until they formed a make-shift set of stairs to the crack that rendered the tower nearly in two. Anwar was first to traverse the steps. His mind raced.

Was Elric still himself?

Had he failed him?

How could he have forgotten about him?

Each step was torture as he felt his breath quicken and his blood pound in his ears; every bit of him was on edge. All the while, the Warlock followed silently behind him.

Anwar could feel himself becoming angry.

Where was their aid? Where had the Warlock been all this time?

He climbed through the crack and into the dark room.

Everything within him was not prepared for what he would see.

CHAPTER 18

He stood still. He didn't know what to do; all he knew is that where Elric had once laid, there now was a husk of a sizzling corpse. He shook his head and turned away.

The Warlock came behind him and walked cautiously to the body.

He didn't say anything as he cast Anwar a look of solemness.

Anwar could feel his eyes brimming up. He wiped with his sleeve.

He forced himself to go towards the corpse. He had to know for sure.

A sudden wave of smell hit him dead in the face.

Lavender and ... lilac?

He turned quicker than a blink as something caught the corner of his eye.

The old wizard sat cross-legged on a conveniently intact chair. Anwar's mouth dropped open. Neither he nor the Warlock had seen him in that dark corner.

"I didn't know you cared so much, Anwar Lioneyes," Elric said with a mirthful glow.

The plague looked to be nowhere on his wrinkled, yet somehow smoother, face. He seemed to be smiling from ear to ear. "You broke the phylactery."

Anwar grabbed him in a rough embrace, nearly toppling him from the chair.

The Warlock stood bewildered as if he were still processing what had just transpired.

Anwar pushed Elric away and gave him a scowl.

"You just let us both walk by you and think you had died!" Elric rubbed his beard.

"Honestly, I didn't know who you both were. You could have been anyone, and seeing as I don't have much magic to spare, I wanted to remain unnoticed until I was sure you were an ally." Anwar sighed but was grateful.

"Old fool."

Elric smiled a toothy grin.

The Warlock gave them both a nod and walked to the edge of the crack before muttering something indistinguishable. The movement grabbed both of their attention. An invisible force surrounded all three of them as quickly as a ripping wind.

Anwar recognized it as something similar to his wards.

The Warlock walked in a half circle for several minutes. He paused and looked at them both.

Anwar remembered the six eyes.

"The lich has five more phylacteries! I broke one of them and one of his eyes stopped glowing."

The Warlock's face looked perplexed.

"It's only possible to have one."

He paced back and forth in place as they watched, only before muttering something to himself and turning back to them.

"I'm glad that both of you are alive and well. There is something now that we must discuss that I don't want anyone else hearing. Thus the reason for all the wards I just cast. I don't have enough magic to teleport us away again, so this will have to do."

He dusted off his arms and leaned towards them.

"The rain was not a natural occurrence. I used nearly all of my strength to call it from the river to the east. It was the last ditch effort on my part to stop the killing of Greyhill's people. Even now the rain draws from my magic. Once this conversation is finished, the rain will stop. It is then that we make haste and leave this place. Please listen to me carefully." "Many escaped today even though it may not have appeared so." He motioned, "Those who have their lives owe thanks to you both. Though even many were spared, even more so have lost their lives." He squatted down.

"I am regretful I could not call the rain quicker, but I had hoped to receive aid from the Archmage and the various leaders of the different branches of mages. That being said, there were none that could come." "None that could come?" Anwar's voice rose with anger.

The Warlock nodded, "Greyhill was not the only place to be attacked today."

Elric raised a brow.

"It seems a war has been declared on all wizards. Plague Souls run rampant among the land. The raven doctors specifically have been targeted and some have been turned into the bird creature that Anwar

had the misfortune of contending with." The Warlock took a long breath, "That I had the fun of dealing with also."

Elric looked between the two. Anwar recognized the look as one who had hundreds of questions but knew it was the wrong time to ask them. “The lich escaped me. It fled into a pillar of smoke before disappearing entirely. Why Greyhill, I do not know. However, the report from the Archmage is that even the kingdom of Jadis was attacked.” The wind around them vibrated.

The Warlock closed his eyes.

“I'm nearly out of magic … but I should be able to continue to monitor the movement of the lich.”

He opened his eyes.

“That is all you need to know for now. We must run. My rain can also detect enemies within it. I can sense that as soon as it goes down that we will be surrounded. It is also likely the plague powder here was not entirely dissolved. The lich didn't want to be followed.”

The rush of wind ceased after the last word left his mouth. He gasped and breathed quickly.

The rain stopped.

Anwar looked between the two of them.

“Time to run,” the Warlock sputtered.

CHAPTER 19

The Warlock rested against the boulder. His face gleamed with a dark twinge.

"That should be far enough."

He dropped down heavily and rested his arms on his knees. Anwar and Elric moved to an overturned log. The wind howled, and each of them looked around every so often to be sure they hadn't been followed.

Elric breathed out a long sigh, closed his eyes, and tilted his head backwards against the moss-covered rock.

"What's the plan?" Anwar asked, leaning forward.

The Warlock chuckled emptily.

"Well, now that we are far enough from Greyhill, the only thing to do now is rest. Once my magic has returned sufficiently, I'll teleport us to my hold. There we can prepare and rest our magic." Anwar nodded.

The last day had exhausted them. They hadn't stopped their quickened pace. There was no knowing where exactly they were, but all they knew was that nothing was chasing them. At least they hoped. None of them had enough magic to verify it, but each of them seemed unnaturally calm. *So this is what no magic felt like.*

Anwar couldn't imagine life without his magicn--much less what a world would be like if the lich overran the realm with his magic eating creatures.

"Will the Archmage declare emergency measures?" Elric asked, interrupting his thought.

The Warlock made an affirmative nod and an "Aye."

"It'll be the first time in hundreds of years."

Anwar clasped his fingers.

"Liches and Plague Souls. Who would have thought …."

"And a gorgon-lich," the Warlock sighed, "That's what the Archmage called the bird creatures."

Elric's eyes opened inquisitively. "Have you any books on them?"

Anwar shook his head.

Elric was always ready to bury his nose into a new book.

He glanced at the old wizard. It was good he still had him to deal with. It was strange to think how often he had taken him for granted. Nearly dying brought perspective.

"Who knows," the Warlock pursed his lips, "This has been a strange age to be alive."

Anwar pulled out the dagger and traced it with his finger. He cringed at how dirty and long his fingernails had become. The Warlock watched him intently.

"That dagger--"

He pointed.

"Is the dagger of Daemos."

He moved his finger along the inscriptions as he realized that there was more to it than he had actually seen. There was a man on it, as well.

The man's eyeline and the dragon's met up as if they were staring at one another.

Anwar held it in his hand out towards the Warlock.

"Keep it." He waved it away, "That blade only works for a specific type of wizard like you. I'm no light wizard. You are." Anwar nodded.

"It chose you. As did the cloak. Keep them both."

He let a mischievous smile spread on his face.

"What?"

"In fact, that cloak was once the Archmage's."

More reverence made him hold it out in front of him and suddenly became aware of how dirty the robe had become.

"He's a light wizard, too?"

Elric seemed surprised at the idea, as well.

The Warlock tucked his head to his chest at the cold wind.

"It's not common knowledge. Light wizards are rare. Daemos was the first to discover light magic and created both of these items to amplify his own magic. In fact it was a direct gift from Daemos to Archmage Protoc. It's only fitting another wizard like you would receive it."

Anwar tightened his grip on the hilt.

"Why did the Archmage not take either of these?" He shrugged.

"Who knows; I was only instructed to guard them until I found someone to whom they responded." He winked, "Don't take it as if you're some chosen one, though. There are more powerful artifacts out there in the realm. It's just these that I happened to have." The Warlock made a strange face.

"I'm not saying you're not important; I'm just saying these are powerful tools to be used to help others. However, they again are just tools. A true wizard is able to use his equipment to enhance instead of being entirely reliant on them. Archmage Protoc knows five types of magic and has mastered them. I know only three and yet still struggle with them. None of which required anything but the depths of our minds." Elric nodded, "Or the depth of pages of a book." The Warlock made a motion with his head.

"Why did Daemos not keep them? The power I felt from the robe and dagger was immense. What became of Daemos?"

Elric cleared his throat, no doubt about to quote a book he had read.

"It's unknown."

The Warlock nodded.

"The last of historical writings say he returned to the realm from which he came ... whatever that means."

Anwar pursed his lips. He had never known Elric to not know something.

The Warlock dusted off his robes and stood up abruptly.

"Ready to go?"

Anwar and Elric made eye contact before agreeing.

"Your magic sure did return quickly."

The Warlock grinned.

"I told you there are many artifacts and magics out in the realm. Maybe I can teach you each soon. Along with maybe even some spells you may not know that will come in handy."

He removed a nearly clear looking stone from his pocket. "This in particular is one such artifact." The wind around them vibrated.

Anwar felt motion sickness in his stomach. The world around them spun and vibrated. It looked like the heavens themselves opened, encircling them. Stars whirled around like they were in a cyclone. In a blink, they were moving throughout colors of blue and purple. It was beautiful magic to be privy to if not for the nausea.

The ground was empty where they once stood. The realm whirled by them as thousands of new spectrums of colors known and unknown blurred his vision. As much as he saw in the short time, it was all taken from them as they stood on the mirrored floor. Elric let out a low whistle.

The Warlock let out a breath.

"So since we are in a safe location now," he said, removing his cloak and tossing it to the floor. It eerily floated to a rack at the opposite side of the room, "I want to prepare for us to journey to Archmage Protoc."

He stopped his movement, and his face paled.

His head jerked back and forth and his hands glowed beside him. He lifted them and an angry harsh look overcame his face. Elric and Anwar jumped at the movement.

"What's wrong?"

The Warlock grimaced.

"Apparently the lich used my tracking spell to pull himself through my teleport magic."

Anwar drew the dagger.

"How is that even possible?" Elric asked.

The Warlock gritted his teeth as he looked around the corridor.

"Any connection can be pulled either way. Like a rope or chain. The lich simply took advantage …." he trailed off. "I can feel him here and I'd guarantee he's not alone."

A blood curdling growl confirmed it.

A loud boom shook the hold.

"How could I be so idiotic?" the Warlock growled.

Another sound boomed followed by dust falling from the ceiling. Multiple shadows encircled them, like darkness dancing amongst a fire. "Be ready," the Warlock whispered.

The shadows grew bigger with each step.

CHAPTER 20

The gorgon-lich lumbered around the corner with a devil grin--or what could be interpreted as one.

A long, forked tongue slithered between the parts of its glimmering beak. The black tar-like muscles convulsed and moved unnaturally in the light of the mirror and candles.

It whispered to itself in an unidentifiable tongue.

Each word made the Warlock wince.

Elric summoned magic by his side. There was a defiant look on his face.

The lich was next to enter the room.

The cracked half of the mask showed the now yellowed skeletal skull. It reached up with its similarly colored fingers and removed it, tossing it to the ground. The mask shattered into hundreds of pieces.

Plague powder snaked along the ground. No doubt that was what it had been made of.

Its mouth hung open and snapped back together in a rough clack. A rutting laugh escaped its mouth.

It pointed as four phylacteries floated from behind it.

The Warlock threw up a ward of clear glass in preparation. The gorgon-lich's claws scraped on the floor almost as if it were impatient.

The lich rutted another laugh as the glass bottles broke. Four of its eyes dimmed into hollow sockets--all except one in the center of its forehead. *One left. But why break almost all of them?*

Elric and Anwar made eye contact.

The green substance swirled and mixed with the plague powder forming into a dense ball of black.

It floated in place in front of the lich.

The lich beckoned with a gesture and the black orb struck into its chest. The creature fell backwards from the impact. It clumsily stood back up as the black powder spread over its bones. Anwar felt his magic pouring into the dagger.

He still wasn't back to his maximum magic, and didn't know how much he would be able to do in this situation. But he thought, three versus two was still a better number.

Crackling green flames arose into orbs in the anatomically correct eye sockets. Curling tree limb like horns jutted from either temple. A fiery green tongue snaked from its open mouth.

All the while, it floated in place as a fine black silk cloak fell over its pointed shoulders.

A singular green glow showed the location of the final phylactery in its chest through the robe.

The lich breathed out a raspy breath.

"M-much B-better," its thin voice whispered.

It moved its fingers and ran them along the robe.

"Now evil has its voice," it cackled.

Its voice deepened with each word.

It pointed.

"Destroy the ward."

The gorgon-lich moved to life and struck the ward with the ferocity of a thunderstorm.

The Warlock grimaced as a long crack moved on its surface.

The bird-like creature squealed with delight.

Anwar's eyes erupted with magic and the dagger was once again the fiery white sword.

The lich tilted its head.

"The light wizard. Clearly not to be underestimated."

It spread its bony fingers as emerald flames ran between them. Elric let loose a shockwave of fire at the lich. The lich lifted its hand to the fireball.

The magical attack shrank as it made contact with its hand and fizzled out into sparks.

The lich cackled.

An arcane blast shot from his hand, smashing into the ward where it made contact--a sizable gaping hole protruded. "The old one should not be, either," it said plainly.

The gorgon-lich shattered the ward at the weak point and barreled into the Warlock.

The Warlock cried out as he pushed away from the monster and engaged in a flurry of magical attacks. Anwar motioned to Elric.

"Help the Warlock."

The lich tilted its head again.

Elric nodded and encased the gorgon-lich in additional magics. Anwar stepped forward as the Warlock almost lost his arm if it had not been for a quick movement to the bird creature. The lich spread out his arms.

"Awful brave of you to face me alone." Anwar gave him a look of disgust.

The lich chanted an unknowable phrase as tendrils of green reached out from its back and grabbed hungrily for him.

Anwar sliced the nearest one clean in half. The tendril burned and made a nasty stench.

The lich cried out as the fire of the sword ran up it and into its back.

It fell to the ground, releasing the other tendrils.

It pushed itself back up to its feet.

It growled dangerously. Despite this, the burning the robe remained intact. The lich whipped its hand to its side and summoned multiple orbs.

They shot past him and whizzed by Anwar. They remained in place beside him and connected into a spider-like web holding him in place. Anwar struggled as the material stuck to him more effectively than glue. He increased the magical flow of his sword and it burned away like kindling.

The lich looked unpleasant.

He dared a look at the gorgon-lich. It continued to be bested by the two wizards. The Warlock had even drawn blood from it. Anwar summoned a fire ball of his own into his free hand.

The lich looked unsettled.

"Catch this," he yelled as he threw it with as much might as he could muster.

The lich moved to stop it but the blast hit it in the center of its chest. It flew backwards with a loud "thwoom."

Its body cracked against the wall and it lay slumped there.

Anwar stood tensely watching the lifeless body.

It stirred after a moment, and slowly stood back up.

It took several deep breaths.

"Even still I cannot best you," it whispered.

Green liquid leaked from its chest, and in its shock it covered it with a hand to stop it.

Anwar noticed that its eyes didn't glow quite as brightly.

The lich's eyes looked behind him at an item that had knocked over in the course of the others' battle. It clacked to the floor. It was the clear stone.

The lich seemed to smile widely as three tendrils snaked around him and headed towards the stone.

Anwar grimaced as he threw the weight of the blade, severing one of the tendrils. The other avoided the slice and grasped the stone firmly in its grip.

The Warlock yelled as he avoided the gorgon-lich, watching the stone moving away from him.

Anwar felt desperation overtake him. He sliced the other tendril in half but was not quick enough to hit the remaining tendril. Elric turned his attention to it but was too slow, also.

The lich opened its free hand and the tendril dropped the stone into it with a dull thump.

Anwar summoned another fire ball and threw it towards the lich.

The creature guarded against the blast this time and shadows encircled it.

"Precisely what I was after."

The lich disappeared in a wave of fire, leaving Anwar floored.

The gorgon-lich melted into nothingness, as the three wizards could only look on in outrage and shock.

CHAPTER 21

The Warlock helped them up as the room was a mess of debris and broken pieces.

No one spoke as they dusted off from the battle.

The lich had escaped.

The Warlock lowered his shoulders and looked away from them. “There’s no telling what’s possible now ....”

Anwar let go of his magic and sheathed the dagger. “Don’t you still have the tracking magic on him?” He shook his head.

“He cleaved that the moment he left. Besides, he won’t be showing his face for some time after that. Even if he has the stone of rejuvenating light, he can’t use it; at least he won’t for some time.” “For some time?”

He nodded.

“It’s likely he means to use it in some way.”

Elric let out a breath and rested against one of the walls, closing his eyes. He had a rip on his side.

“We are lucky to have made it out of that with our lives. Not many others

I’d wager could boast the same.”

The Warlock rolled up his sleeves.

"Gather any magical items that aren't broken. This place isn't safe anymore."

Anwar nodded; as much as he wanted to do that, there didn't seem to be much that was of any use in this particular room. The fight had left only a few sparse objects, which included a hat, some wands, and several crystals.

Elric slid down the wall into a sit.

"You all right, old man?"

He nodded.

"Too old for all this."

After a time of salvaging what they could, the Warlock prepared to teleport them.

"Honestly, I haven't a clue as to where to go from here. It is likely nowhere is safe enough, but I know we need to find the Archmage and let him know about what transpired here." They both agreed.

"Are you ready to go?"

"Where to?"

The Warlock gave an uncharacteristic shrug.

"I'm open to suggestions. Anywhere I have in mind has been overrun with those monsters."

"What about Jadis?"

The Warlock rubbed his temple.

"To Jadis we go then."

The room began to spin around them as their bodies traversed the magical spell.

To Jadis it was.

TO BE CONTINUED IN BOOK 2.

A NOTE FROM THE AUTHOR:

I wanted to take this opportunity to make a heartfelt thank you to all my readers and supporters. You truly make writing fun with all of your reactions and questions. As long as you keep reading, I will keep writing. My goal for this book is to write a few novellas based on interest. I am in love with telling stories and weaving new and exciting adventures for readers.

Please continue to support me on this platform by telling friends and family about my books! This helps me to continue to pursue my dream of becoming a full time author.

Please consider following me on Facebook on my Author Page:

Author M. W.Fenn, Instagram: Fenn_Matthew or consider my Podcast:

TheAshenbornAuthor. Anything helps! Thank you for reading and I look forward to more adventures with you!

-Author M. W.Fenn

www.ingramcontent.com/pod-product-compliance
Lightning Source LLC
LaVergne TN
LVHW041110150826
845673LV00007B/1991

* 9 7 9 8 6 6 3 2 5 2 4 7 8 *